PETER PAN

PETER PAN

JAMES M. BARRIE

Retold by
Susan Shebar

Illustrated by
T. Lewis

Troll Associates

Library of Congress Cataloging in Publication Data

Shebar, Susan E.
    Peter Pan.

    Summary: The adventures of the three Darling
children in Neverland with Peter Pan, the boy who
would not grow up.
    [1. Fantasy]   I. Barrie, J.M. (James Matthew),
1860-1937. Peter Pan.   II. Lewis, T. (Thomas), ill.
III. Title.
PZ7.S53814Pe   1988   [Fic]   87-15480
ISBN 0-8167-1199-2 (lib. bdg.)
ISBN 0-8167-1200-X (pbk.)

Wendy, John, and Michael Darling were fast asleep in their bedroom. Their parents had already left for a party. Nana, the family dog, slept near the garden in the yard. All was quiet in the Darling house this night.

Suddenly, the bedroom lights blinked, then went out. An instant later, another light shone in the room. It was a small, brilliant light—a hundred times stronger than regular light.

The tiny light dashed about the room, then came to rest. Moments later, the window blew open wide. A boy dropped through it into the room. He was dressed in green with leaves for a shirt. The tiny light dashed past the boy, flew about the room, and then disappeared inside a jug.

"Tinker Bell," the boy called softly. "Do come out and help me look for my shadow."

A tiny tinkle of golden bells flowed up from the jug. For the light inside the jug was not a light at all. It was a fairy no bigger than your hand.

Tinker Bell flew out of the jug and sat on the big chest. The boy jumped onto the chest too. When he did, something came tumbling out of one of the drawers. There on the floor lay the boy's shadow. The boy whooped with delight. He was so excited that he slammed the chest drawer closed, trapping Tinker Bell inside.

The boy stepped on his shadow, thinking it would stick to him. But it did not stick. When he saw a bar of soap on the wash basin, he grabbed it, rubbing it on his feet. Then he stood up and stepped on his shadow again. It still would not stick. He stamped his foot and began to cry. His sobs woke Wendy. She sat up.

"Who are you?" Wendy asked, clearly startled.

The boy rose to his feet and bowed politely. "I am Peter Pan, and I have come for my shadow."

"Well," Wendy said slowly, "you can't put your shadow on that way. I guess I could sew it on for you."

As Wendy sewed, Peter Pan told her how he had come to lose his shadow.

"I often visit this room," he said. "I sit in the open window and listen to your mother when she tells her wonderful stories. But one night, after you and the boys were asleep, your mother saw me. I flew away, but my shadow caught on a nail and tore off."

"There—all finished," Wendy said, snipping the last bit of string from the shadow. "You shouldn't be peeking in people's windows, you know. Besides, doesn't your mother tell you stories?"

Peter stood and lifted his foot. His shadow sprang to life. It was still a bit wrinkled, but it did everything Peter did.

"I don't have a mother," he said.

"No mother?" Wendy asked sadly. "Then how do you live? Where do you live?"

"Second star to the right," Peter said. He was pointing out the window. "And I'm all right. I ran away when I heard my mother and father talking about what I should be when I grew up. I never want to grow up. I want to stay a boy and have fun. So now I live in Neverland with the Lost Boys."

Just then, Peter noticed Tinker Bell was missing. Where was she? He sprang to the top of the chest. "Tink, are you in there? Come out and meet Wendy."

The drawer shook, and there was a faint tinkle of bells. But the fairy would not come out. She did not like the attention Peter was giving Wendy.

Wendy was delighted. "Peter," she cried, "you don't mean to tell me there is a fairy in this room!"

Peter pulled the drawer open and Tinker Bell flew out. She brushed past Peter's hand. Fairy dust sprinkled across his fingers. Wendy had to bend down to get out of Tinker Bell's way.

"Peter, who are the Lost Boys?" Wendy asked.

"They are the boys who fell out of their baby carriages when their parents were looking the other way. If they are not claimed in seven days, they are sent to Neverland. I am their captain."

"What fun it must be!"

"Yes," said Peter. "But we are lonely too. And we have no one to tell us stories." Then Peter had an idea. "Wendy, do come with us and tell stories to the Lost Boys, Tink, and me."

"Oh, I can't," Wendy said quickly. "Think of my brother John and baby Michael."

Peter scratched his head, then he brightened. "Bring them too," he said.

"But Peter, I can't fly."

"I'll teach you! It's easy," Peter said.

"Will you teach John and Michael too?"

"Of course," Peter said. He sprang into the air.

Wendy ran to John and Michael to wake them.

"Wake up!" she cried. "Peter Pan has come. He's going to teach us to fly!"

John rubbed his eyes and sat up. "I say, Peter, can you really fly?"

Peter flew around the room.

"Wow!" said Michael.

"Your turn," Peter said.

The three children jumped on their beds, spread their arms, and tried to fly. But they all went down instead of up.

Peter laughed. "No, no," he said.

"How do you do it?" John asked, rubbing his knees.

"Think lovely thoughts, and the thoughts will lift you into the air."

The children tried again. Each thought the loveliest thought they could think. But not one of them started to fly. Peter scratched his head again. Then he remembered. No one can fly without fairy dust. Peter still

TRAIN

had Tinker Bell's fairy dust on his fingers. He clapped his hands in delight, then sprinkled each of the children with a bit of it.

"Now, think lovely thoughts and wiggle your shoulders this way," he said, wiggling his. "And let go."

Michael was the first to try. He thought of large ice-cream cones and wiggled his shoulders. All at once he was in the air. John thought of slaying a fierce dragon. Suddenly, he was in the air also. Wendy closed her eyes. She thought how lovely it would be to fly. When she opened her eyes, she was nearly on the ceiling!

"Look at us!" they cried. Up and down and around they went, swooping, gliding, and giggling.

"And now," Peter said, "are you ready to come with me to meet the Lost Boys of Neverland?"

John and Michael looked at Wendy. She was the oldest of the Darling children. She made all of the important decisions.

"Do let's go, Wendy. Please!" John pleaded. "It does sound like fun."

"Yes, yes, I want to go too," Michael added. Wendy hesitated. Peter hopped onto the windowsill.

"There are mermaids," he said. "And pirates."

"Pirates! Let's go at once!" John cried.

It was just at that moment that Mr. and Mrs. Darling returned home from the party. They would have reached the bedroom in time to stop the children if it had not been for Tinker Bell. She warned Peter to be quick. Peter called to the children.

"Not a moment to lose!" He soared out into the starlit sky with Tinker Bell, Wendy, John, and Michael close behind. Their dog, Nana, woke in time to see the children fly out of the window. She yelped and barked at the children, but they did not hear her as they flew away into the night.

"Second star to the right and straight on till morning," Peter said, urging them on.

The children flew the whole night, through the dark heavens and the wispy clouds. They weaved in and out of the twinkling stars.

Early in the morning the children could see whales far below in the sea. Peter flew down and rode on a whale's back. The whale spouted water through his blowhole. The children laughed and Peter splashed in the spray.

Michael had begun to grow tired and fell asleep. Down he dropped toward the cold, dark sea. Peter laughed. But Wendy was afraid. "Save him!" she cried.

Peter stopped laughing. He dove down through the air toward the falling baby. Michael had almost reached the water when Peter swooped under him and lifted him up. Michael woke with a start.

"There it is, Neverland at last!" said Peter, pointing ahead. "Just follow the arrows."

The children looked all around. A million golden arrows glittered above their heads. They all pointed toward the island called Neverland. Wendy could see beautiful mermaids swimming in the bay. Soon the arrows faded, however. A gloomy mist covered part of the island where a ship sat in the water.

Peter turned toward the children. "There are pirates asleep on the ship below us. If you like, we can go down and fight them."

John grew very excited. "I say, who is their captain?" he asked.

"Hook," Peter answered. His face grew stern. He hated Captain James Hook.

"What is he like? Is he big?"

"Well, he is not as big as he once was," Peter said proudly. "I cut off his hand and threw it in the sea. It was eaten by a crocodile."

"Oh, my," John said, quite amazed. "Then he can't fight now?"

"Oh, can he ever!" Peter said. "He has an iron hook instead of a right hand. He uses it like a claw." Peter grew serious. "There is one thing that every boy who serves under me must promise. If we meet Hook in an open fight, you must leave him to me."

The boys quickly agreed. They shook hands. Peter turned to face the bay below and began to fly down toward it. Peter did not know that some of the pirates were still awake. They had seen him in the sky and had pointed their big gun, Long Tom, up at him. Suddenly, the cannon blasted. The shot missed. But the exploding force of air blew Peter, John and Michael far out to sea. Wendy and Tinker Bell were blown upward. The two became separated from the others.

Tinker Bell flew back and forth close to Wendy. Her tiny bell tinkled and fairy dust filled the air. Wendy thought Tinker Bell was her friend, so she followed the fairy's lead. But Tinker Bell was jealous of Wendy. She was trying to think of a way to get rid of the girl.

Far below, in Neverland, the Lost Boys heard the sound of Long Tom. They knew that Captain Hook used the gun only on Peter Pan. And so the six Lost Boys went out looking for Peter. First, there was Tootles. He had a sweet, kind nature. Nibs was happy and lighthearted, while Slightly thought a great deal of himself. Curly was always in some sort of trouble. And the twins stayed close together.

The Indians who lived on the island were also loyal to Peter Pan. Peter had once saved their princess, Tiger Lily, from the evil pirates. When the Indians heard the big gun, they went out searching for the pirates. The pirates, in turn, were out searching for the Lost Boys. Everyone was circling the island. But no one met because they were all going the same way at the same time.

Suddenly, the Lost Boys heard the pirates approach from a distance. As fast as they could, the Lost Boys ran through the forest to the seven largest trees. Each one had a hole big enough for any of the boys or Peter to slip through. The holes were entrances to the underground home Peter and the Lost Boys shared. Quickly, then, the six Lost Boys disappeared down the tree holes. But before they did, a pirate saw Nibs running through the woods.

"Shall I go after him, Captain?" he asked.

"Not now," Hook said. "I want to catch the six of them and their leader too. Fan out and look for them all."

The pirates were a mean gang. And none was meaner among them than Captain Hook. He was tall and thin. His hair hung in long, dark curls. And instead of a right hand, he had an iron hook with a very sharp point.

Hook turned to the pirate he trusted most, Smee. Hook talked about Peter Pan.

" 'Twas he who cut off my hand, Smee, and flung it to a crocodile. That crocodile liked the taste of my hand. He has been following me ever since, licking his lips. Now he's waiting to eat the rest of me."

Hook sat on a mushroom. He took a deep breath and sighed. There was a quiver in his voice.

"Smee," he said, "that crocodile would have had me before now. But by a lucky chance it swallowed a clock that goes tick-tick inside it. Whenever it comes close, I hear the tick and run away."

"Someday," said Smee, "the clock will run down, and then he will get you."

Hook wetted his lips. "Aye," he said. "That's the fear that haunts me."

Hook's seat began to feel warm. He stood up. "Smee, this mushroom is hot."

Hook and Smee looked carefully at the huge mushroom. There was something strange about it. They stretched their arms around the mushroom and pulled hard. It popped out of the ground with a jolt. Stranger still, smoke began to pour out of the hole in the ground. The pirates looked at each other.

"A chimney!" they both exclaimed. Hook put his ear close to the chimney. He could hear children's voices.

"Smee, it's the Lost Boys," Hook whispered.

All the pirates returned to listen. Then they replaced the mushroom. Hook stood for a long time, thinking.

"Return to the ship," he said at last to his men. "Bake a large rich cake. Make it chocolate with green sugar on it. We will bring it back here where the boys will find it. They will gobble it up because they do not have a mother to tell them that too much cake will make them sick. Then we will catch them!" All the pirates burst into laughter.

Through their laughter, however, they could hear a small sound. It came from the stream in the forest. It moved closer toward the mushroom chimney, closer toward the pirates, closer toward Captain Hook. *Tick-tick-tick-tick!* Hook turned pale and trembled. His teeth began to rattle in his mouth.

"The crocodile!" he gasped. Hook turned and ran as fast as he could out of the woods and to his waiting ship.

Not long after the pirates left, the Lost Boys decided to search for Peter Pan again. They began to spread out in all directions. But Nibs called them back together.

"Hurry," he called. "I have seen a great bird. It is flying this way. And as it flies, it calls 'Poor Wendy!' It must be a Wendy bird!"

The boys were very excited. They had never seen a Wendy bird. Tinker Bell flew down among the boys. She had a plan.

"Peter wants you to shoot the Wendy bird," she said.

The boys looked at each other. They never questioned their captain's orders. Tootles had a bow and arrow with him. He took out the arrow and placed it on the bow. He drew the string back, then stopped.

Tinker Bell could hardly wait.

"Quick, Tootles, quick!" she screamed. "Peter will be so pleased."

"Out of the way," Tootles shouted. He fired. The arrow soared into the air and struck Wendy in her chest. Wendy fluttered and fell onto the hard ground. She lay very still.

Tinker Bell flew over the boys. She laughed, then flew into the forest to hide. The boys crowded around Wendy.

Soon they heard Peter calling to them.

"Great news, boys," he cried. "At last I have brought a mother for you all. Her name is Wendy. Have you seen her? I believe she flew this way."

The boys looked stricken.

"Peter," Tootles said slowly, "a terrible thing has happened, and we are very sorry."

They stood back. Peter saw Wendy lying on the ground. John and Michael began to cry.

"Whose arrow?" Peter asked sternly.

Tootles fell to his knees. "Mine, Peter," he said.

Peter pulled the arrow out of Wendy's chest. He raised it above Tootles, holding it like a dagger. Tootles did not move.

"Strike, Peter," he said.

"I cannot strike," Peter said. "Something is holding my arm back."

Suddenly, Nibs cried out, "Look! It's Wendy! Wendy is alive!"

Wendy smiled up at Peter. Peter bent down. Carefully, he lifted Wendy into his arms and carried her into his underground home. For the next several days, Peter, the Lost Boys, John, and Michael nursed Wendy back to health.

Wendy, John, and Michael loved the underground home. It had one large room with a dirt floor. Growing up from it were large mushrooms that the boys used as stools. A fireplace warmed the room. One bed stood against the back wall.

At six-thirty every night, Wendy pulled the bed down. It almost filled the room. All of the boys would hop onto the bed. Wendy would tell stories until they fell asleep.

Tinker Bell had finally come home. She was very sorry for what she had tried to do to Wendy. Wendy understood and forgave her.

One night, Wendy settled down to tell a story. Michael, John, and the Lost Boys were in bed. Peter sat on a mushroom stool with Tinker Bell on his shoulder. As Wendy prepared to tell her story, pirates crept through the woods above. They wanted to catch the Indians. Slowly, they circled the Indian village and waited for the sign to attack.

"There was once a gentleman and a lady," Wendy began. "Their names were Mr. and Mrs. Darling. They had three children—John, Michael, and Wendy. They had a dog named Nana. One night, Peter Pan flew into their house. He taught the children how to fly. And he told them about the Lost Boys in Neverland."

The boys in the bed smiled.

"The children wanted to meet the Lost Boys. So, Peter, Tink, and the children flew away to Neverland."

Now came the part Peter hated.

"The children knew their mother and father would always keep the window open for them to fly back," continued Wendy. "And so the children stayed in Neverland for many years and had a happy time."

Peter could stand no more of the story. He jumped up and stamped his feet.

"A lot you know about mothers," he said. "I thought my mother would always keep the window open for me too. But when I tried to go home, I found the window was closed and locked. There was another boy sleeping in my bed. I couldn't go home again, not ever."

Wendy, John and Michael grew afraid.

"We must go home at once," Wendy said. "Peter, will you make the arrangements?"

Peter was surprised, then angry. He didn't know his words would make the children leave. He didn't want Wendy to go home.

"No, I won't," he said coldly.

Wendy looked hurt. Peter felt sorry for her.

"Tinker Bell can take you across the sea if you really want to do it," he said slowly.

Wendy looked at the Lost Boys. They were sad to be losing their only mother.

"If you will all come to our home, I'm sure my father and mother will let you live with us," she said.

The Lost Boys jumped for joy. "Peter, can we go?"

"All right," Peter said with a bitter voice. "But I will not go with you. I'm going to stay in Neverland. I never want to grow up. I'm going to stay a boy and have fun."

Wendy and the boys begged Peter to go with them. But he refused.

"It's all right," Wendy said at last. "Peter knows the way to the window. He can come whenever he wishes to see us again."

Tinker Bell and the children gathered their things for the trip. One by one they said good-bye to Peter. They each made their way up through the hole to the ground above their home.

All of a sudden, loud shouts and cries filled the air. The children rushed back underground.

"Peter, what is it?" Wendy asked. The noise had frightened them.

"The pirates have attacked the Indians!" Peter said. "Everyone stay quiet, and listen. If the Indians have won, they will beat the tom-tom. That's always their victory signal."

Above ground, the pirates' attack took the Indians by surprise. Most of the tribe was captured. Princess Tiger Lily and a few Indian braves escaped through the dark woods.

Smee searched the Chief's tepee until he found the tom-tom. Captain Hook was delighted. He and Smee crept quietly through the forest to the mushroom chimney. Smee beat the tom-tom twice, then stopped to listen. They both pressed their ears close to the chimney.

Down below the boys heard the sound of the drum. "The Indians have won!" Peter shouted.

The children cheered. It would now be safe to leave for home.

Hook signaled to his men. The pirates quickly surrounded the seven trees where Wendy and the boys would come up out of their underground home.

"Think of it, Smee," whispered Hook. "We'll get them all, and we didn't have to give them a cake."

The first to come out of a tree was Curly. He poked his head out of the tree hole and looked around. All of a sudden, a huge pirate clamped his hand over Curly's mouth. A second pirate picked him up and threw him to another, who tossed him to another, until Curly landed on the ground at Hook's feet. Nibs was captured next, then Slightly, then Tootles, and then the twins.

John was the first of the Darling children to come above ground. He too was captured and waited helplessly for Michael to join him.

Wendy was the last to be captured. Hook took off his hat and bowed to her. She tried to scream and warn Peter, but Smee clamped his hand tightly over her mouth. Just then, music from Peter's pipes started to come up through the hole in the tree.

"You see, my dear," Hook sneered, "Peter has forgotten you already."

Wendy tried to bite Smee's hand, but he was too strong for her. Hook laughed and ordered his men to take the captives to his pirate ship. Then Hook rushed to the mushroom chimney and looked inside.

Below ground, Peter played on his pipes. He tried to make believe that he did not care about Wendy and the boys. But he felt so sad and lonely that his head began to hurt. Peter took a bottle of medicine from a shelf. He poured a bit of it into a glass. But he hated to take medicine, so he put it down. At last, he lay down on the bed and forced himself to sleep.

When Hook was sure that Peter was asleep, he lowered himself through the hole and into the underground house. Silently, he tiptoed to the sleeping Peter Pan. Then he caught sight of the medicine glass and reached into the pocket of his coat for a small vial of black liquid. Hook pulled out the cork and poured five drops from the vial into Peter's glass. He took one long, gloating look at Peter, then slinked back up the tree.

Peter slept for a long time. Just as he was starting to awaken, he heard a small tinkle of bells. "Hi, Tink," he said lazily. "You finally have what you always wanted, Tink. You and I are alone in Neverland."

Tink began to fly wildly around the room. Peter watched and listened carefully as Tinker Bell told him about the capture of Wendy and the boys.

Peter sprang to his feet, grabbing his weapons. He dashed toward the hole that would lead him above ground. But the medicine glass caught Peter's eyes. "Just a minute, Tink," he said. "I'd better drink this first."

"No!" Tink rang her bells loudly. She had overheard Hook talking about his deed. "Something is wrong," she said.

"Don't be silly, Tink. What could be wrong?" He raised the glass to his lips.

Tink panicked. With lightning speed she flew between Peter's lips. When he tipped the glass, Tink drank the medicine before it could reach Peter's mouth. A few moments later, her body began to shake. With Peter's help, she flew to the bed and lay down.

"It was poisoned, Peter." Her voice was growing weak.

Peter knelt beside her. "Oh, Tink!" he cried. "Think beautiful thoughts and the thoughts will help you."

But Tinker Bell's light was growing dimmer. Peter tried shaking her. But it didn't help. He was afraid. If Tinker Bell's light went out, she would die.

He searched all over the house, but he couldn't find anything that would help Tink. Suddenly, he had an idea. Peter stood up as tall as he could reach, his arms spread out wide.

"Boys and girls of the world!" he called. "Everyone who has ever dreamed of Neverland, please help Tinker Bell live! If you believe in Tinker Bell," he shouted, "clap your hands. Don't let Tink die!"

Peter waited. Then he heard a loud sound. It was far away, but soon it came closer and closer. At last Neverland was filled with the thunderous clapping of millions of children all over the world.

It worked! Tink's light grew brighter. Her voice grew strong. All at once, she leaped from the bed and flitted around the room! Fairy dust sparkled in the air!

Peter shouted his thanks to all the children who had helped Tinker Bell. "And now," he vowed, raising his sword, "to save the others."

Peter pressed through the dark, silent forest toward the bay. "It's Hook or me this time, I swear!" he shouted.

aptain Hook walked along the deck of his ship. He was happy. He had captured most of the Indians, and he had the three Darling children and all the Lost Boys.

"Ready the plank and bring the boys up from the brig!" he shouted to Smee.

The pirate did as he was told, and brought the boys up on deck. He bound their legs together with chains, locking them with a big brass lock.

"All right, boys," Hook said. "You can join me and my crew—or you can die. You first, John. What will it be?"

John drew himself up tall. "We'll not die. I say, Peter Pan will save us."

Hook let out a long, cruel laugh. "By this time," he told them, "Peter is lying dead, all alone in his great big bed."

"You liar!" Michael shouted. He tried to run to strike Hook, but the chain pulled tight around his legs. He fell to the deck with a thud.

Hook laughed again. He ordered John to walk the plank. John stood at the edge of the plank but would not walk on it. Hook grew angry.

"Bring up Wendy!" he shouted.

Smee and the pirates pulled Wendy up on deck. They tied her to the mast. Her shoulders began to shake.

Hook thought she must be cold. He decided to have a bit of fun and pretended to be kind. So he ordered one of the pirates to fetch his very own cape and cover Wendy so that she would be warm.

The boys tried to look brave for Wendy. But deep inside, they were scared.

"Now, boys, what will it be? Join me or walk the plank?
If you refuse to do either, you will see Wendy die first."
"No!" Michael screamed. The Lost Boys shook.
Wendy stood very still. "Be brave," she whispered.

Hook began to move toward Wendy. She took a deep breath. Michael and John gasped. Just as Hook reached Wendy, he heard a sound. *Tick-tick-tick-tick!*

Hook's eyes flashed open wide. His teeth began to chatter and his knees began to shake.

"The crocodile!" he shouted. "Hide me! Hide me!"

The pirates followed Hook down the gangway and deep into the hold of the ship. Within a few seconds, only the children were left on deck. The boys hopped to the side of the ship. They wanted to see the crocodile that had eaten Hook's hand.

The crocodile was not there. But Peter Pan was. He sprang out of hiding. Peter was making a wonderful ticking noise. The boys wanted to shout to him, but Peter stopped them.

"Quiet, boys," he said. "It's Hook or me this time. Don't spoil it now."

The boys moved back and waited for Peter's orders. Peter grabbed his sword. He climbed the side of the cabin and looked about. He could see a pirate coming toward him.

"Ready now," he whispered. "Here comes the first one."

The pirate came up on deck. Peter jumped on him and struck him. John clasped his hands over the pirate's mouth to keep him quiet. The man fell forward. Four of the Lost Boys caught him before he could hit the deck. When Peter waved his hands, the boys threw the pirate overboard. There was a splash, then silence. One by one, five more pirates came on deck. One by one, Peter and the boys threw them overboard.

Soon, all was quiet. Peter slipped into Hook's cabin. Hook wasn't there. But Peter found a large brass key. He quietly crept on deck and opened the lock on the boys' chains. He signaled the boys to find any weapons they could, and to hide.

Peter sprang to Wendy's side. He took the cape off her shoulders and cut the ropes that held her. He quietly told her to hide with the boys. When she was safely hidden, Peter covered himself with the cape and stood leaning against the mast. Then he took a deep breath and crowed as loudly as his voice could yell.

"It's Peter Pan!" Hook screamed from down in the hold. The rest of the pirates rushed on deck. The deck was empty. Only the caped figure could be seen.

"Well, missy," one of the pirates said, "there's no one here but you now."

"There's one," the caped figure said.

"Who's that?"

"Peter Pan, the avenger!" came the answer. Peter flung off his cape. The pirates fell back in surprise. "Down and at them!" cried Peter to the boys.

In a moment, the ship was alive with the clash of swords. If the pirates had stayed together, they might have won. But they were not good fighters and they were afraid of Peter Pan. They ran here and there, letting themselves be easy targets for the boys. Some of the pirates jumped overboard into the sea. Some tried to hide in dark corners, but John and Michael found them.

At last, the fighting stopped. But suddenly, Captain Hook himself came rushing onto the deck. His long, sharp sword flashed in his one good hand. The boys surrounded him at once. Hook swung his sword at one boy after another. Each boy jumped back just in time to miss its edge.

Peter sprang into the middle of the fight. "This man is mine," he cried. Peter swung his own sword about his head. The boys stepped back to watch him fight.

Hook now stood face to face with Peter. Peter's eyes narrowed. He swung his sword slowly from side to side. Hook sneered and let loose his meanest laugh. Suddenly, he jabbed at Peter, but Peter jumped out of the way and flew to another part of the deck.

Hook was angry. "Stay put!" he shouted.

Now it was Peter's turn to laugh. He leaped down onto the deck, throwing Hook off balance. But Hook spun around and swung at Peter. Their swords clashed. The sound of metal hitting metal rang loudly in the air. Peter laughed again, then swung his sword again at Hook. On and on they fought, each poking and jabbing and swinging his sword at the other.

Once more Peter lunged at Hook, this time knocking the sword from Hook's hand. Peter smiled.

"So, Hook. At last I have you at my mercy."

Peter bowed low, kicked the sword close to Hook, and told him to pick it up. Hook sprang for the weapon, and the battle was on again.

"I am youth. I am joy," Peter cried.

Hook fought as hard as he could. But Peter fluttered around him and always stayed just outside his reach. Again and again, Peter darted in and pricked Hook's arm or his leg. Hook knew that he could not fight much longer. Then Peter raised his sword and jumped through the air at Hook.

Hook sprang to the bulwarks. "You won't have me today!" he shouted.

Suddenly, Hook leaped overboard into the sea. There was a splashing and thrashing noise next to the ship. Hook screamed, then all was silent. In a moment, a soft *tick-tick-tick-tick* could be heard swimming away from the ship.

"So," Peter said, "the crocodile has finally eaten all of Captain James Hook." John, Michael, the Lost Boys, and Wendy gathered around Peter, cheering.

"All right," he said. "The ship is ours. Turn her about and head for home!"

The night was very still in the Darling home. It was close to the end of summer, and there was a slight chill in the air. Mr. Darling thought there was a draft coming from the children's bedroom. He went into the room to close the window. But Mrs. Darling stopped him. She wanted the window to stay open. It reminded her of her children before they had disappeared.

Mrs. Darling looked around the room. She had come into the bedroom again and again, hoping to see her three children back in their beds. But each time, she found the beds empty. She sat down on Wendy's bed and breathed a sigh. Mr. Darling sat down next to her. He put his arm around her to make her feel better. Their dog, Nana, walked slowly into the room. Her head was bent down. She also missed the children.

Mr. and Mrs. Darling still did not know what had happened to their children. The last time they saw Wendy, John, and Michael was just before leaving for the party. All three were sound asleep in their beds. When Mr. and Mrs. Darling returned, their children were gone.

Nana had tried to tell them that Wendy, John, and Michael flew away into the night. But dogs couldn't talk. And children couldn't fly, or so Mr. and Mrs. Darling believed.

"All we can do is wait and hope," Mr. Darling said.

"Yes," Mrs. Darling said with a sad voice. "Wait, hope, and keep the window open."

They sat together for a long time. They were both thinking of the children. Finally, they grew tired. It was time to go to bed. Mr. and Mrs. Darling stood up slowly. "Come, Nana," Mrs. Darling said. "No sense waiting in here tonight."

Nana rose sadly and followed the Darlings out of the room.

"Quick," Peter said as he and Tinker Bell dropped to the floor through the open window. "I thought they would never leave. Come on now, Tink. Help me close the window. When Wendy arrives, she will see the window closed and locked. She will think that her mother and father have closed her out. Then she will lead the boys back to Neverland and stay with us forever."

Peter and Tinker Bell had a hard time pushing the window closed. It had remained open so long that some of the hinges had become stuck. Peter heard Nana bark.

"Quick, Tink. The big dog is coming back!"

Peter and Tinker Bell pushed as hard as they could. At last, the window moved. Peter and Tink flew out the window, then shut it tight from the outside.

Nana came bouncing and barking to the room. Mrs. Darling ran in after her. At once, she rushed over to the window and opened it. She thought the window must have closed by itself, although she could not think of how that could have happened. She tied the window back with heavy rope so that it would not close again.

Peter saw her sit on John's bed. Very soon, he saw two tears roll down her cheeks. She bent down and laid her head on her arms.

"She's crying," Peter said. "She really does love her children. She wants them to come home."

Tinker Bell shook her bells sadly.

"Come on, Tink. Let's go away from the window." And so they flew away, over the roof and out of sight.

At last, Mr. Darling came into the bedroom. He turned out the lights and led Mrs. Darling and Nana back to their own beds.

Many hours passed. The house was quiet. But just before daybreak, Wendy, John and Michael flew through the bedroom window. They were tired from their long flight. They wondered why Tinker Bell had left them before they were halfway across the sea. Still, they were very excited to be home at last. Wendy heard Nana barking downstairs in the kitchen.

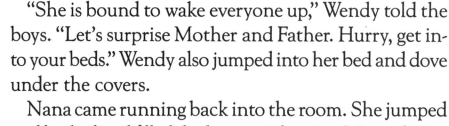

"She is bound to wake everyone up," Wendy told the boys. "Let's surprise Mother and Father. Hurry, get into your beds." Wendy also jumped into her bed and dove under the covers.

Nana came running back into the room. She jumped and barked and filled the house with noise. Mr. and Mrs. Darling came dashing in to see what all of Nana's noise was about.

Wendy jumped out of bed. "Mother! Father!" she cried.

"It's Wendy!" Mother screamed. At first she thought it was a dream.

John jumped up. "Hello, everyone. It's fun to be back."

"It's John!" Father cried, but he could hardly believe his eyes.

Nana rushed over to Michael's bed and pulled the covers back. She began to bark wildly.

"It's me!" Michael shouted.

They all stretched their arms out wide and ran to each other. They hugged and kissed until they were all too tired to hold onto each other anymore. All the while, Peter Pan and Tinker Bell went unnoticed. They were outside the window, looking in.

"Oh, Mother, Father," Wendy said when she could catch her breath at last, "we have such news to tell you!"

"Yes, yes," John and Michael said. "We have been to Neverland. We have lived with Peter Pan and Tinker Bell and the Lost Boys. We have seen Indians and fought with pirates!"

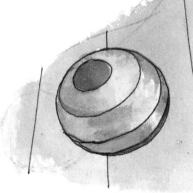

"Yes," said Wendy. "We saw mermaids and whales too. And we met the lovely Indian Princess, Tiger Lily."

Mr. and Mrs. Darling could hardly believe all they were hearing. "Who are the Lost Boys?" they asked.

"Oh, goodness," Wendy said and ran to the door. "I almost forgot. They are boys who live in Neverland. Their home is in a big hole under the ground."

"They all sleep in one bed, and they have mushrooms for chairs," Michael said.

"And we have brought them home with us," John said excitedly.

Mr. and Mrs. Darling stared at the children. "But their parents will worry about them."

"They have no mother and father," Wendy said.

"Humph," said Peter, who was still looking in at the window. "They have me!"

Mr. Darling looked at his wife. "Well," he said slowly, "six more children will be a lot of children."

Mrs. Darling smiled. "Yes, I know. But come on, let's go and meet them."

The Darling children cheered. John and Michael rushed out of the room. They each wanted to be the first to tell the Lost Boys that they were going to stay and live with the Darling family forever.

Suddenly, Wendy heard a tap at the window. Not until Nana and her parents had left the room did she go to the window and look out.

"Hello, Peter. Hello, Tinker Bell. I wondered what happened to you. Will you two come and live with us?"

Peter shook his head. "No," he said. "I never want to grow up. I want to live in Neverland and have fun."

"Oh," Wendy said sadly, "then you have come to say goodbye." She found it hard to say goodbye to Peter.

"Don't forget me," Peter said.

"I'll never forget you, Peter," said Wendy. Tears filled her eyes. "The window will always be open for you."

Peter Pan smiled and waved goodbye. Tinker Bell shook her tiny bells in farewell. Fairy dust fell as she did. Wendy watched until they were completely out of sight. Then she went downstairs to join her family, leaving the window open behind her.

	DATE DUE		

F   Barrie, James M.
BAR   Peter Pan

DORLING KINDERSLEY ⊞K EYEWITNESS BOOKS

WORLD
WAR I

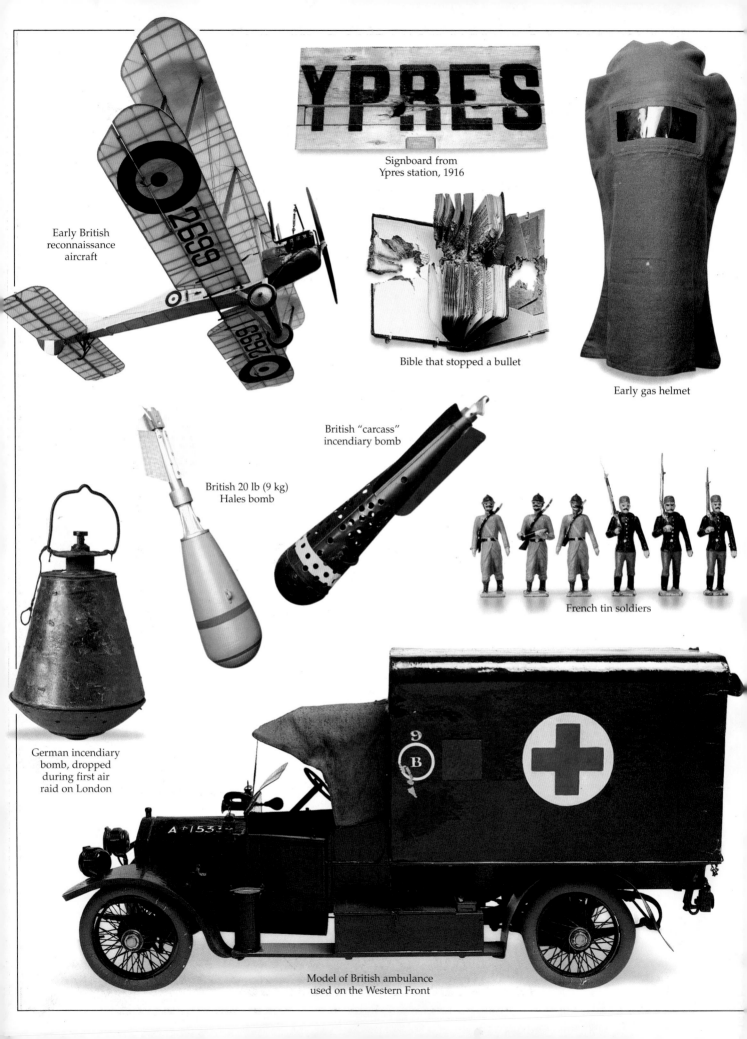

Early British
reconnaissance
aircraft

Signboard from
Ypres station, 1916

Bible that stopped a bullet

Early gas helmet

British "carcass"
incendiary bomb

British 20 lb (9 kg)
Hales bomb

French tin soldiers

German incendiary
bomb, dropped
during first air
raid on London

Model of British ambulance
used on the Western Front

DK EYEWITNESS BOOKS

WORLD WAR I

Prussian Iron
Cross

US Distinguished
Service Cross

Written by
SIMON ADAMS

Photographed by
ANDY CRAWFORD

British Maxim mark 3
machine-gun

Caricature puzzle of
Herbert Asquith,
British prime
minister from
1908–1916

Figurine of Grand
Duke Nicolas,
Commander-in-
Chief of the
Russian armies at
the start of the war

DK
A Dorling Kindersley Book

IN ASSOCIATION WITH
THE IMPERIAL WAR MUSEUM

British officer's compass

German steel helmet adapted for use with a telephone

Dummy rifles used by British army recruits 1914–15

Dorling  Kindersley

LONDON, NEW YORK, SYDNEY, DELHI, PARIS, MUNICH and JOHANNESBURG

Project editor Patricia Moss
Art editors Julia Harris, Rebecca Painter
Senior editors Monica Byles, Carey Scott
Senior art editors Jane Tetzlaff, Clare Shedden
Category publisher Jayne Parsons
Managing art editor Jacquie Gulliver
Senior production controller Kate Oliver
Picture research Sean Hunter
Jacket designer Dean Price
US editors Gary Werner, Margaret Parish

This Eyewitness ® Guide has been conceived by Dorling Kindersley Limited and Editions Gallimard

First American Edition, 2001

03 04 05 10 9 8 7 6 5

Published in the United States by
DK Publishing, Inc.
375 Hudson Street,
New York, NY 10014

Library of Congress Cataloging-in-Publication Data

Adams, Simon, 1955–
    World War I / written by Simon Adams ; photographed by Andy Crawford. -- 1st American ed.
        p. cm. -- (Eyewitness guides)
    Includes index.
ISBN 0-7894-7939-7 -- ISBN 0-7894-7940-0 (pbk.)
1. World War, 1914-1918--Juvenile literature. [1. World War, 1914-1918.] I. Crawford, Andy, ill. II. Title. III. Series.

D521.7 .A33 2001
940.3--dc21
                                                                2001028512

Color reproduction by
Colourscan, Singapore
Printed in China by
Toppan Printing Co., (Shenzhen) Ltd.

See our complete catalog at
www.dk.com

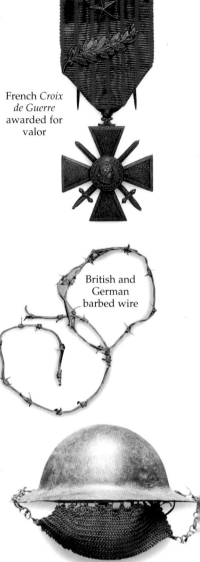

French *Croix de Guerre* awarded for valor

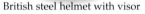

British and German barbed wire

British steel helmet with visor

Grenade

German orderly's medical pouch

Contents

High explosive
shells

Divided Europe

AT THE START of the 20th century, the countries of Europe were increasingly hostile to each other. Britain, France, and Germany competed for trade and influence overseas, while Austria-Hungary and Russia both tried to dominate the Balkan states of southeast Europe. Military tension between Germany and Austria-Hungary on the one hand and Russia and France on the other led to the formation of powerful military alliances. A naval arms race added to the tension. In 1912-13, two major wars broke out in the Balkans as rival states battled to divide Turkish-controlled lands between them. By 1914, the political situation in Europe was tense, but few believed that a continental war was inevitable.

HMS DREADNOUGHT
The launch of HMS *Dreadnought* in February 1906 marked a revolution in battleship design. With its 10 12-inch (30-cm) guns and a top speed of 21 knots, the British ship outperformed and outpaced every other battleship of the day. As a result, Germany, France, and other maritime nations began to design and build their own "Dreadnoughts," starting a worldwide naval armaments race.

KAISER WILHELM II
Wilhelm II became emperor of Germany in 1888, when he was just 29. He had a withered arm and other disabilities, but overcame them through his strong personality. As emperor, he tried to turn Germany from a European power into a world power, but his aggressive policies and arrogant behavior upset other European nations, particularly Britain and France.

Some children had models of HMS Dreadnought *and could recite every detail of her statistics*

Hand-painted, tinplate toy battleship

EUROPEAN RIVALRIES
In 1882 Germany, Austria-Hungary, and Italy signed the Triple Alliance to protect themselves against invasion. Alarmed by this, France and Russia formed an alliance in 1894. Britain signed ententes (understandings) with France in 1904 and Russia in 1907. During the war, Serbia, Montenegro, Belgium, Romania, Portugal, and Greece fought with the Allies. Bulgaria and Turkey fought alongside Germany and Austria-Hungary – the Central Powers. Italy joined the Allies in 1915.

Central Powers

Allied Nations

Neutral

A FAMILY AFFAIR?
Although George V and Czar Nicholas II look very similar, they were not directly related. Nicholas's wife, Alexandra, however, was a cousin of George V, as was Emperor Wilhelm of Germany.

Czar Nicholas II of Russia   George V of Britain

THE GERMAN FLEET
In 1898, Germany began an ambitious naval building program designed to challenge the supremacy of the British Royal Navy. While German admirals commanded these new ships in the Baltic and North seas, German children played with tin battleships in their bathtubs.

Key to wind-up motor

THE POWER HOUSE
The factory, shown above, in the Ruhr valley of western Germany belonged to the Alfred Krupp Arms Company. The Krupp family was the largest arms supplier in the world. Germany was a largely agricultural nation when it became a united country in 1871. Over the next 30 years, new iron, coal, steel, engineering, and shipbuilding industries turned Germany into the third biggest industrial country in the world, after the US and Britain, which were the largest.

The fatal shot

THE ASSASSINS
Gavrilo Princip, above right, fired the fatal shot. He belonged to the Black Hand terrorists, who believed that Bosnia should be part of Serbia.

ON JUNE 28, 1914, the heir to the Austro-Hungarian throne, Archduke Franz Ferdinand, was assassinated in Sarajevo, Bosnia. Bosnia had been part of Austria-Hungary since 1908, but it was claimed by neighboring Serbia. Austria-Hungary blamed Serbia for the assassination, and on July 28 declared war. What began as the third Balkan war rapidly turned into a European war. Russia supported Serbia, Germany supported Austria-Hungary, and then France supported Russia. On August 4, Germany invaded neutral Belgium on its way to France. It intended to knock France out of the war before turning its attention to Russia, thus avoiding war on two fronts. But Britain had guaranteed to defend Belgium's neutrality, and it, too, declared war on Germany. The Great War had begun.

MOBILIZE!
During July 1914, military notices were posted up across Europe informing citizens that their country's army was being mobilized (prepared) for war and that all those belonging to regular and reserve forces should report for duty.

THE AUSTRO-HUNGARIAN ARMY
The Austro-Hungarian empire had three armies – Austrian, Hungarian, and the "Common Army." Ten main languages were spoken! The official one was German, but officers had to learn their men's language, leading to frequent communication difficulties. The complex structure of the army reflected Austria-Hungary itself, which in reality was two separate monarchies ruled by one monarch.

GERMANY REJOICES
Germany prepared its army on August 1, declaring war against Russia later the same day and against France on August 3. Most Germans in the cities were enthusiastic for the war, and many civilians rushed to join the army in support of Kaiser and country. Germans in the countryside were less enthusiastic.

Austro-Hungarian *Reiter* (Trooper) of the 8th Uhlan (Lancer) Regiment

First bomb bounced off canopy and landed under following car

Archduke and his wife Sophie sat in the back of the open-top car

Princip fired at close range from the running board

ONE DAY IN SARAJEVO
The six assassins – five Serbs and one Bosnian Muslim – lay in wait along Archduke Ferdinand's route to the Austrian governor's residence in Sarajevo. One of them threw a bomb at Ferdinand's car, but it bounced off and exploded under the following car, injuring two army officers. The Archduke and his wife went to visit the injured officers in the hospital 45 minutes later. When their car took a wrong turn, Gavrilo Princip stepped out of the crowd and shot the couple. Ferdinand's wife died instantly, and he died 10 minutes later.

June 28 Archduke Franz Ferdinand is assassinated in Sarajevo.
July 5 Germany gives its ally, Austria-Hungary, total support for any action it takes against Serbia.

July 23 Austria issues a drastic ultimatum to Serbia, which would undermine Serbian independence.
July 25 Serbia agrees to most of

Austria-Hungary's ultimatums, but still mobilizes as a safety precaution.
July 28 Austria-Hungary ignores Serbia's readiness to seek a peaceful

end to the crisis and declares war.
July 30 Russia mobilizes in support of its ally, Serbia.
July 31 Germany demands Russia stops its mobilization

Bekanntmachung.

Mobilmachung befohlen.

Erfter Mobilmachungstag, der 2. August

Vorſtehender Allerhöchſter Befehl wird hierdurch öffentlich bekannt gemacht.

Berlin, den 1. Auguſt 1914.

Der Oberbürgermeiſter
Wermuth.

German (above) and French (right) mobilization posters

ARMÉE DE TERRE ET ARMÉE DE MER

ORDRE DE MOBILISATION GÉNÉRALE

Par décret du Président de la République, la mobilisation des armées de terre et de mer est ordonnée, ainsi que la réquisition des animaux, voitures et harnais nécessaires au complément de ces armées.

Le premier jour de la mobilisation est le *Dimanche deux Août 1914*

VIVE LA FRANCE
The French army mobilized on August 1. For many Frenchmen, the war was an opportunity to seek revenge for the German defeat of France in 1870–71 and the loss of Alsace-Lorraine to German control.

ALL ABOARD!
The German slogans on this westbound train read "Daytrip to Paris" and "See you again on the Boulevard," as all Germans believed that their offensive against France would soon take them to Paris. French trains heading east toward Germany carried similar messages about Berlin.

> *"The lamps are going out all over Europe"*
>
> SIR EDWARD GREY
> BRITISH FOREIGN SECRETARY, 1914

August 1 Germany mobilizes against Russia and declares war; France mobilizes in support of its ally, Russia; Germany signs a treaty with Ottoman Turkey; Italy declares its neutrality.
August 2 Germany invades Luxembourg and demands the right to enter neutral Belgium, which is refused.

August 3 Germany declares war on France.
August 4 Germany invades Belgium on route to France; Britain enters the war to safeguard Belgian neutrality.
August 6 Austria-Hungary declares war on Russia.
August 12 France and Britain declare war on Austria-Hungary.

War in the west

CHRISTMAS TREAT
The London Territorial Association sent each of their soldiers a "Christmas pudding" in 1914. Other soldiers received gifts in the name of Princess Mary, daughter of King George V.

EVER SINCE THE 1890s, Germany had feared that it would face a war on two fronts – against Russia in the east and against France, Russia's ally since 1893, in the west. Germany knew the chances of winning such a war were slim. By 1905, the chief of the German staff, Field Marshal Count Alfred von Schlieffen, had developed a bold plan to knock France swiftly out of any war before turning the full might of the German army against Russia. For this plan to work, the German army had to pass through Belgium, a neutral country. In August 1914, the plan went into operation. German troops crossed the Belgian border on August 4, and by the end of the month, invaded northern France. The Schlieffen Plan then required the army to sweep around the north and west of Paris; but the German commander, General Moltke, modified the plan and instead headed east of Paris. This meant his right flank (side) was exposed to the French and British armies. At the Battle of the Marne on September 5, the German advance was held and pushed back. By Christmas 1914, the two sides faced stalemate along a line from the Belgian coast in the north to the Swiss border in the south.

IN RETREAT
The Belgian army was too small and inexperienced to resist the invading German army. Here, soldiers with dog-drawn machine guns are withdrawing to Antwerp.

IN THE FIELD
The British Expeditionary Force (BEF) had arrived in France by August 22, 1914. Its single cavalry division included members of the Royal Horse Artillery, whose L Battery fired this 13-pounder quick-firing Mark I gun against the German 4th Cavalry Division at the Battle of Néry on September 1. This held up the German advance into France for one morning. Three gunners in the battery received Victoria Crosses for their valor.

Steel helmet

Third gunner fires the gun on command

Second gunner loads the shell

First gunner hands shell to second gunner on command

Shaft to attach gun to horses that pull the gun

Soldiers wore puttees, long strips of cloth wrapped around their legs

THE CHRISTMAS TRUCE

On Christmas Eve 1914, soldiers on both sides of the Western Front sung carols to each other in comradely greeting. The following day, troops along two-thirds of the front observed a truce. All firing stopped, and church services were held. A few soldiers crossed into no-man's-land to talk to their enemy and exchange simple gifts of cigarettes and other items. Near Ploegsteert Wood, south of Ypres, Belgium, a game of soccer took place between members of the German Royal Saxon Regiment and the Scottish Seaforth Highlanders. The Germans won 3–2. In some places, the truce lasted for almost a week. A year later, however, sentries on both sides were ordered to shoot anyone attempting a repeat performance.

Soldier shooting at enemy with a note saying "Christmas Eve – Get em!"

British and German soldiers greeting each other on Christmas Day

EYEWITNESS

Captain E.R.P. Berryman, of the 2nd Battalion 39th Garwhal Rifles, wrote a letter home describing the truce. He told his family that the Germans had put up Christmas trees in their trenches. This cartoon illustrates the absurdity of his situation – shooting the enemy one day and greeting them as friends the next.

German trench

Rope wrapped around recoil mechanism

Fires 12.5 lb (5.6 kg) shells a distance of 5,900 yards (5,395 m)

HEADING FOR THE FRONT

The German advance into northern France was so rapid that by early September, its troops were along the Marne River, only 25 miles (40 km) east of Paris. General Gallieni, military governor of Paris, took 600 taxis and used them to convey 6,000 men to the front line to reinforce the French 6th Army.

Fighting men

THE OUTBREAK OF WAR in Europe in August 1914 changed the lives of millions of men. Regular soldiers, older reservists, eager recruits, and unwilling conscripts all found themselves caught up in the war. Some of them were experienced soldiers, but many had barely held a rifle before. In addition to the European forces, both Britain and France drew heavily on armies recruited from their overseas colonies and from the British dominions. The design and detail of their uniforms differed considerably, although brighter colors soon gave way to khaki, dull blue, and gray.

France

GRAND DUKE NICOLAS
At the outbreak of war, the Russian army was led by Grand Duke Nicolas, uncle of Czar Nicholas II. In August 1915, the czar dismissed his uncle and took command himself. As commander-in-chief, the czar dealt with the overall strategy of the war. The Russian armies were led by generals who directed the battles. The other warring countries employed similar chains of command.

Hat flaps could be pulled down to keep out the cold

Jerkin could b made of goat- or sheepskin

Ammunition pouch

Woolen puttees wrapped around shins

THE BRITISH ARMY
At the start of war, the British army contained 247,432 regulars and 218,280 reservists. Soldiers wore a khaki uniform consisting of a single-breasted tunic with a folding collar, trousers, puttees or leggings worn to protect the shins, and ankle-boots. In the winter, soldiers were issued with additional items such as jerkins. Many wore knitted scarves and balaclavas sent from home.

Lee Enfield Rifle

British soldier

Thick boots to protect feet

EMPIRE TROOPS
The British and French armies included large numbers of recruits from their colonial possessions in Africa, Asia, the Pacific, and the Caribbean. In addition, the British dominions of Australia, New Zealand, Canada, and South Africa sent their own armies to take part in the conflict. Many of these troops had never left their home countries before. These Annamites (Indo-Chinese), above from French Indo-China were stationed with the French army at Salonika, Greece, in 1916. They wore their own uniforms rather than those of the French army.

EASTERN ALLIES
In Eastern Europe, Germany faced the vast Russian army, as well as smaller armies from Serbia and Montenegro. In the Far East, German colonies in China and the Pacific Ocean were invaded by Japan. These illustrations come from a poster showing Germany's enemies.

Russia

France   Britain   Belgium

WESTERN ALLIES

In Western Europe, Britain, France, and Belgium were allied against Germany. The British and French armies were large, but the Belgian army was small and inexperienced. These illustrations come from a German poster identifying the enemy.

Steel helmets were issued in 1916

Field tunic (Waffenrock)

Tent cloth

Cartridge pouch

Mauser rifle

Stick grenade

Gas mask

German soldier

French infantrymen photographed in 1918

THE FRENCH ARMY

The French army was one of the largest in Europe. Including reservists and colonial troops, the French army totaled 3,680,000 trained men at the outbreak of war.

Water bottle

Haversack with personal items

Lebel rifle

French infantryman, known as *le poilu*

THE GERMAN ARMY

The German army was the strongest in Europe because it had been preparing for war. At the outbreak of hostilities, it consisted of 840,000 men. All men under the age of 45 were trained for military service and belonged to the reserve army. On calling up the reserves, the German army could expand to over four million trained men.

Russia   Serbia   Montenegro   Japan

Enlisting

AT THE OUTBREAK OF WAR, every European country but one had a large standing army of conscripted troops ready to fight. The exception was Britain, which had a small army made up of volunteers. On August 6, 1914, the Secretary of War, Lord Kitchener, asked for 100,000 new recruits. Whole streets and villages of patriotic men lined up to enlist. Most thought they would be home by Christmas. By the end of 1915, 2,446,719 men had volunteered, but more were needed to fill the depleted ranks of soldiers. In January 1916 conscription was introduced for all single men aged 18–41.

WAR LEADER
British Prime Minister Herbert Asquith was caricatured as "the last of the Romans" and replaced by David Lloyd George in December 1916.

THE TEST
Every British recruit had to undergo a medical test to make sure he was fit to fight. Large numbers failed this test, because of poor eyesight, chest complaints, or general ill health. Others were refused because they were under 18, although many lied about their age. Once he passed the test, the recruit took the oath of loyalty to the king and was then accepted into the army.

"YOUR COUNTRY NEEDS YOU"
A portrait of British War Minister General Kitchener was used as a recruiting poster. By the time it appeared in late September 1914, though, most potential recruits had already volunteered.

Small box respirator gas mask

Haversack contained the filter of the small box respirator

Pouch contained three clips, each of which held five bullets

Two sets of five ammunition pouches on belt

LINE UP HERE FOR KING AND COUNTRY
At the outbreak of war, long lines formed at recruiting offices around the country. Men from the same area or industry grouped together to form the famous Pals battalions, so they could fight together. By mid-September, half a million men had volunteered to fight.

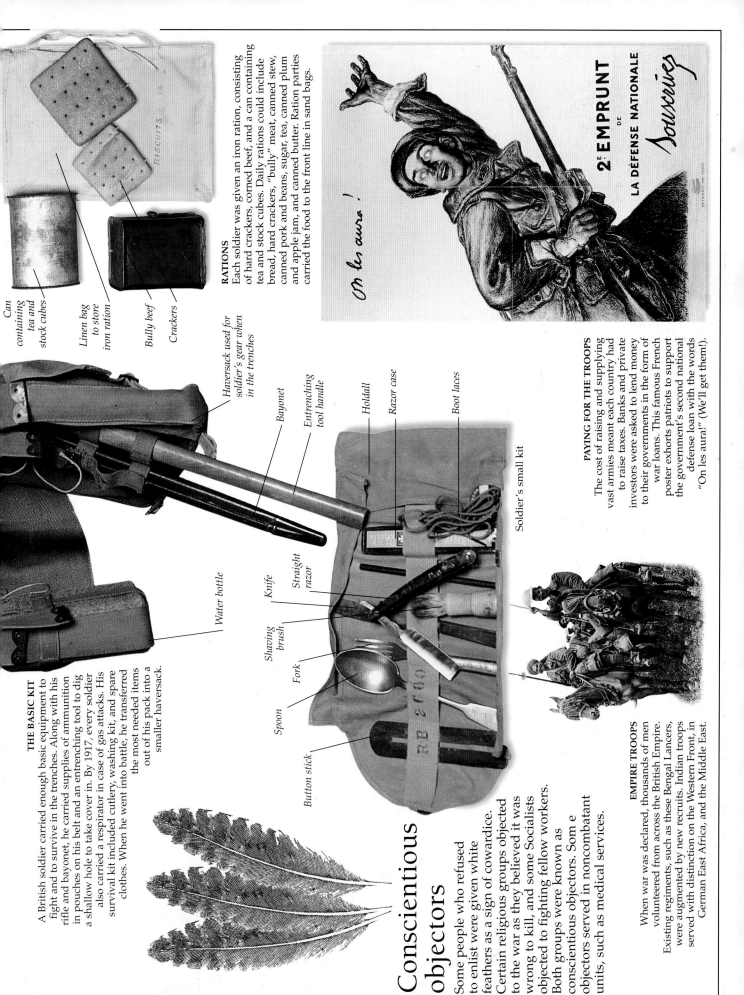

RATIONS

Each soldier was given an iron ration, consisting of hard crackers, corned beef, and a can containing tea and stock cubes. Daily rations could include bread, hard crackers, "bully" meat, canned stew, canned pork and beans, sugar, tea, canned plum and apple jam, and canned butter. Ration parties carried the food to the front line in sand bags.

Can containing tea and stock cubes

Linen bag to store iron ration

Bully beef

Crackers

On les aura !

2ᴱ EMPRUNT DE LA DÉFENSE NATIONALE Souscrivez

THE BASIC KIT

A British soldier carried enough basic equipment to fight and to survive in the trenches. Along with his rifle and bayonet, he carried supplies of ammunition in pouches on his belt and an entrenching tool to dig a shallow hole to take cover in. By 1917, every soldier also carried a respirator in case of gas attacks. His survival kit included cutlery, washing kit, and spare clothes. When he went into battle, he transferred the most needed items out of his pack into a smaller haversack.

Haversack used for soldier's gear when in the trenches

Bayonet

Entrenching tool handle

Holdall

Razor case

Boot laces

Water bottle

Knife

Straight razor

Shaving brush

Fork

Spoon

Button stick

Soldier's small kit

RB 2600

PAYING FOR THE TROOPS

The cost of raising and supplying vast armies meant each country had to raise taxes. Banks and private investors were asked to lend money to their governments in the form of war loans. This famous French poster exhorts patriots to support the government's second national defense loan with the words "On les aura!" (We'll get them!).

EMPIRE TROOPS

When war was declared, thousands of men volunteered from across the British Empire. Existing regiments, such as these Bengal Lancers, were augmented by new recruits. Indian troops served with distinction on the Western Front, in German East Africa, and the Middle East.

Conscientious objectors

Some people who refused to enlist were given white feathers as a sign of cowardice. Certain religious groups objected to the war as they believed it was wrong to kill, and some Socialists objected to fighting fellow workers. Both groups were known as conscientious objectors. Some objectors served in noncombatant units, such as medical services.

Digging the trenches

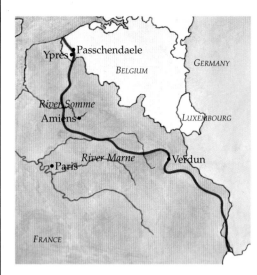

THE FRONT LINE
By December 1914, a network of trenches stretched along the Western Front from the Belgian coast in the north down through eastern France to the Swiss border, 400 miles (645 km) in the south. By 1917, it was possible in theory to walk the entire length of the front along the winding trench network.

━━━ Front line of trenches

AT THE OUTBREAK OF WAR, both sides on the Western Front expected to take part in massive military maneuvers over hundreds of miles of territory, and to fight fast-moving battles of advance and retreat. No-one expected a static fight between two evenly matched sides. A stalemate occurred mainly because powerful long-range artillery weapons and rapid-fire machine guns made it dangerous for soldiers to fight in unprotected, open ground. The only way to survive such weapons was to dig defensive trenches.

Blade cover

THE FIRST TRENCHES
Early trenches were just deep furrows, which provided minimal cover from enemy fire. These troops from the 2nd Scots Guards dug this trench near Ypres in October 1914. Their generals believed that such trenches were only temporary, as the "normal" war of movement would resume in the spring.

ENTRENCHING TOOLS
Each soldier carried an entrenching tool. With it, the soldier could dig a scrape – a basic protective trench – if he was caught in the open by enemy fire. He could also use it to repair or improve a trench damaged by an enemy artillery bombardment.

American M1910 entrenching tool

SIGNPOSTS
Each trench was signposted to make sure no one lost his way during an attack. Nicknames frequently became signposted names.

POSITIONING THE TRENCH
Neither side had great expertise in digging trenches at the outbreak of war, but they quickly learned from their mistakes. The Germans usually built trenches where they could best observe and fire at the enemy while remaining concealed. The British and French preferred to capture as much ground as possible before digging their trenches.

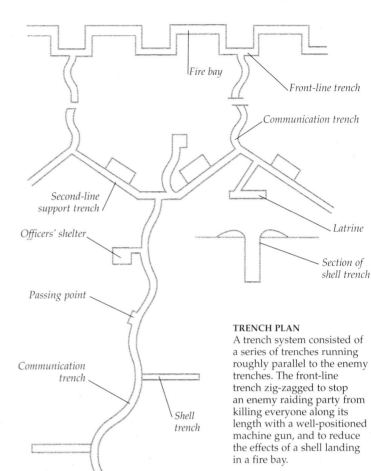

BOARDED UP
One of the main dangers of trench life was the possibility of being buried alive if the walls collapsed. By summer 1915, many German trenches were reinforced with wooden walls to prevent this from happening. They were also dug very deep to help protect the men from artillery bombardments.

HOME SWEET HOME?
The Germans constructed very elaborate trenches because, as far as they were concerned, this was the new German border. Many trenches had shuttered windows and even doormats to wipe muddy boots on! Allied trenches were much more basic because the Allies expected to recapture the occupied territory.

Fire bay

Front-line trench

Communication trench

Second-line support trench

Latrine

Officers' shelter

Section of shell trench

Passing point

Communication trench

Shell trench

TRENCH PLAN
A trench system consisted of a series of trenches running roughly parallel to the enemy trenches. The front-line trench zig-zagged to stop an enemy raiding party from killing everyone along its length with a well-positioned machine gun, and to reduce the effects of a shell landing in a fire bay.

COPING WITH THE MUD
Rain, snow, and natural seepage soon filled trenches with water. Wooden slats, known as duckboards, were laid on the ground to keep soldiers' feet reasonably dry, but the constant mud remained one of the major features of trench life.

Life in the trenches

Daytime in the trenches alternated between short periods of intense fear, when the enemy fired, and longer periods of boredom. Most of the work was done at night when patrols were sent out to observe and raid enemy trenches, and to repair their own front-line parapets and other defenses. Dawn and dusk were the most likely times for an enemy attack, so all the troops "stood to," or manned the fire bays, at these times. The days were usually quiet, so the men tried to catch up on sleep while sentries watched the enemy trenches. Many soldiers used this time to write home or keep a diary of events. There were no set mealtimes on the front line, and soldiers ate as and when transportation was available to bring food to the front by carrying parties. To relieve the boredom, soldiers spent one week to 10 days on the front line, then moved into the reserve lines, and finally went to a rear area to rest. Here, they were given a bath and freshly laundered clothes before returning to the trenches.

A LITTLE SHELTER
The trenches were usually very narrow and often exposed to the weather. The Canadian soldiers in this trench have built a makeshift canopy to shelter under. The sides are made of sandbags piled on top of each other.

Soldier removing mud from ammunition pouch with a piece of cloth

A RELAXING READ?
This re-creation from London's Imperial War Museum shows a soldier reading. While there was plenty of time for the soldiers to read during the day, they were often interrupted by rats scurrying past their feet and itching lice in their clothes.

NEAT AND CLEAN
The cleaning of gear and the waterproofing of boots was as much a part of life in the trenches as it was in the barracks back home. These Belgian soldiers cleaning their rifles knew that such tasks were essential to maintaining combat efficiency.

OFFICERS' DUGOUT
This re-creation in London's Imperial War Museum of an officers' dugout on the Somme in the fall of 1916 shows the cramped conditions people endured in the trenches. The officer on the telephone is calling in artillery support for an imminent trench raid, while his weary comrade is asleep behind him on a camp bed. Official notices, photographs, and postcards from home are tacked around the walls.

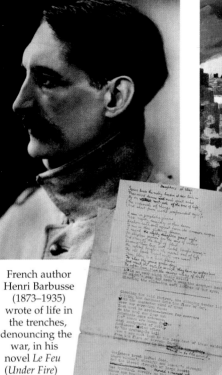

French author Henri Barbusse (1873–1935) wrote of life in the trenches, denouncing the war, in his novel *Le Feu* (*Under Fire*) of 1916.

Poem and self portrait by the British poet and artist Isaac Rosenberg (1890–1918)

The Menin Road (1918) by Paul Nash

Artists and poets

Some soldiers used their spare time in the trenches to write poems or make sketches. A huge number wrote long letters home or kept a diary. After the war, many of these writings were published. Literary records of trench life made fascinating and shocking reading. In 1916, the British government began to send official war artists, such as Paul Nash (1889–1946), to the front to record the war in paint.

Paints and brushes belonging to the British artist Paul Nash

CAVE MEN
Ordinary soldiers – such as these members of the British Border Regiment at Thiepval Wood on the Somme in 1916 – spent their time off duty in "funk holes," holes carved out of the side of the trench, or under waterproof sheets. Unlike the Germans, the British did not intend to stay in the trenches too long, so did not want the soldiers to make themselves comfortable.

TRENCH CUISINE
These French officers are dining well in a reserve trench in a quiet area. Others were less fortunate, enduring canned food or mass-produced meals cooked and brought up from behind the lines and reheated in the trench.

Soldiers served alongside a regiment of rats and lice

Ready to fight

It's easy to imagine that most of the action on the Western Front took place when soldiers left their trenches and fought each other in open ground, no-man's land, between the two opposing front lines. In reality, such events were far rarer than the constant battle between soldiers in their facing lines of trenches. Both armies took every opportunity to take shots at anyone foolish or unfortunate enough to be visible to the other side. Even soldiers trying to rescue wounded comrades from no-man's land or retrieve bodies caught on the barbed-wire fences were considered fair targets. Raiding parties from one front line to the other added to the danger. This relentless war of attrition kept every soldier on full alert, and meant that a watch had to be kept on the enemy lines every hour of the day.

PREPARE TO FIRE
These German troops on the Marne in 1914 are firing through custom-built gun holes. This enabled them to view and fire at the enemy without putting their heads above the parapet and exposing themselves to enemy fire. Later on in the war, sandbags replaced the earthen ramparts. On their backs, the troops carry leather knapsacks with rolled-up greatcoats and tent cloths on top.

IN CLOSE QUARTERS
Soldiers were armed with a range of close-combat weapons when they went on raiding parties in case they needed to kill an enemy. The enemy could be killed silently so that the raiding soldiers did not draw attention to themselves. The weapons were rarely used.

French trench knife

German stick grenade

German club

German timed and fused ball grenade

British Mills bomb

WRITING HOME
Canon Cyril Lomax served in France in 1916–17 as a chaplain to the 8th Battalion Durham Light Infantry. As a noncombatant, he had time to describe in illustrated letters home the horrors he encountered. The armies of both sides had chaplains and other clergy at the front.

Last time over the bags was rather terrible. The few who managed to pull themselves out of the waist-deep mud had to stand on the top & pull others who were stuck out of the trenches. Imagine doing that with machine guns hard at work, to say nothing of snipers. One man I know of was drowned in the mud. Another was only extricated by eight men. Naturally no supports or rations could come up, & after gaining their objectives in some cases, in others being mown down at once they had to retire.
I have had to make this trench too wide

WALKING WOUNDED

This re-creation in London's Imperial War Museum shows a wounded German prisoner being escorted by a medical orderly from the front line back through the trench system to a regimental aid post. Many, however, were not so fortunate. A soldier wounded in no-man's land would be left until it was safe to bring him back to his trench, usually at night. Many soldiers risked their lives to retrieve wounded comrades. Sadly, some soldiers died because they could not be reached soon enough.

REGIMENTAL AID POST

Battalion medical officers, as shown in this re-creation from London's Imperial War Museum, worked through the heat of battle and bombardment to treat the flood of casualties as best they could. They dressed wounds, tried to relieve pain, and prepared the badly wounded for the uncomfortable journey out of the trenches to the field hospital.

Path of bullet

ALWAYS IN ACTION

This photograph of Bulgarian soldiers was taken in 1915. It shows that soldiers could never let their guard down while in a trench. A permanent look out must be kept, and guns always primed and ready in case the enemy mounted a sudden attack. The soldiers had to eat in shifts to ensure constant readiness for battle.

SAVED BY A BOOK

The soldier carrying this book was lucky. By the time the bullet had passed through the pages, its passage was slowed enough to minimise the injury it caused.

"The German that I shot was a fine looking man ... I did feel sorry, but it was my life or his"

BRITISH SOLDIER JACK SWEENEY, NOVEMBER 21, 1916

Communication and supplies

FIELD TELEPHONE
Telephones were the main communication method between the front line and headquarters. They relayed voice and Morse code messages.

British night signal

GETTING IN TOUCH
Teams of engineers – such as this German group – were trained to set up, maintain, and operate telephones in the field. This allowed closer and more regular contact between the front line and HQ than in previous wars.

Communicating with and supplying front-line troops is the biggest problem faced by every army. On the Western Front, this problem was particularly acute because of the length of the front line and the large number of soldiers fighting along it. In mid-1917, for example, the British army required 500,000 shells a day, and million-shell days were not uncommon. To supply such vast and hungry armies, both sides devoted great attention to lines of communication. The main form of transportation remained the horse, but increasing use was made of mechanized vehicles. Germany made great use of railroads to move men and supplies to the front. Both sides set up elaborate supply systems to ensure that front-line troops never ran out of munitions or food. Front-line troops also kept in close touch with headquarters and other units by telephone and wireless.

MISSILE MESSAGES
Enemy fire often cut telephone lines, so both sides used shells to carry written messages. Flares on the shells lit up to signal their arrival. Signal grenades and rockets were also widely used to convey prearranged messages to front-line troops.

Message rolled up in base

German message shell

French army pigeon handler's badge

Canvas top secured with ropes

LOAD NOT TO EXCEED 3 TONS

WD

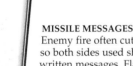

POSTAL PIGEON
Carrier pigeons were often used to carry messages to and from the front line where telephone lines did not exist. But the noise and confusion of the front meant that the birds easily became bewildered and flew off in the wrong direction. Germany used "war dogs" specially trained to carry messages in containers on their collars.

Soldier getting a lift to the front on a supply wagon

Supply trucks heading for the front

TWO-WAY TRAFFIC

One of the main problems on the Western Front was the lack of good roads to and from the front line. Quiet country lanes suddenly became major thoroughfares as columns of marching men, supply trucks, munitions wagons, field ambulances, and other vehicles forced their way through. The traffic was frequently two-way, with soldiers ready for combat marching to the front, passing their tired and often wounded comrades heading in the opposite direction.

Wounded British troops returning from the trenches in November 1916

WHEEL POWER

Both sides used trucks and vans to ferry men and supplies to the front line. This British 3-ton Wolseley transport truck was specially built for war service, but other smaller trucks and vans were also used.

Sides dropped down for access

Open driver's cab

British Wolseley 3-ton transport truck

FABULOUS BAKER GIRLS

Behind the lines, vast quantities of food were produced every day to feed the soldiers at the front. British kitchens, cafeterias, and bakeries, such as this one in Dieppe, France, were often staffed by members of the Women's Army Auxiliary Corps (W.A.A.C.) The Corps was set up in February 1917 to replace the men needed to fight on the front line. Women also played a major role as clerks, telephone operators, and storekeepers, ensuring that the front line was adequately supplied and serviced at all times.

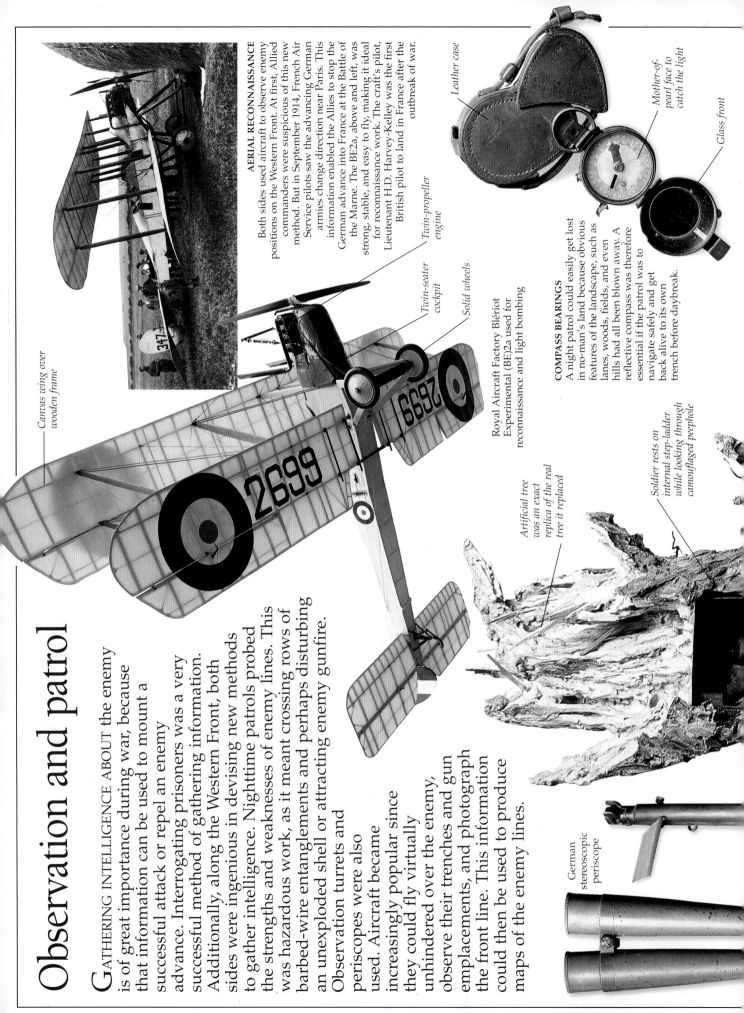

Observation and patrol

GATHERING INTELLIGENCE ABOUT the enemy is of great importance during war, because that information can be used to mount a successful attack or repel an enemy advance. Interrogating prisoners was a very successful method of gathering information. Additionally, along the Western Front, both sides were ingenious in devising new methods to gather intelligence. Nighttime patrols probed the strengths and weaknesses of enemy lines. This was hazardous work, as it meant crossing rows of barbed-wire entanglements and perhaps disturbing an unexploded shell or attracting enemy gunfire. Observation turrets and periscopes were also used. Aircraft became increasingly popular since they could fly virtually unhindered over the enemy, observe their trenches and gun emplacements, and photograph the front line. This information could then be used to produce maps of the enemy lines.

AERIAL RECONNAISSANCE
Both sides used aircraft to observe enemy positions on the Western Front. At first, Allied commanders were suspicious of this new method. But in September 1914, French Air Service pilots saw the advancing German armies change direction near Paris. This information enabled the Allies to stop the German advance into France at the Battle of the Marne. The BE2a, above and left, was strong, stable, and easy to fly, making it ideal for reconnaissance work. The craft's pilot, Lieutenant H.D. Harvey-Kelley was the first British pilot to land in France after the outbreak of war.

Canvas wing over wooden frame

Twin-propeller engine

Twin-seater cockpit

Solid wheels

Royal Aircraft Factory Blériot Experimental (BE)2a used for reconnaissance and light bombing

Leather case

Mother-of-pearl face to catch the light

Glass front

COMPASS BEARINGS
A night patrol could easily get lost in no-man's land because obvious features of the landscape, such as lanes, woods, fields, and even hills had all been blown away. A reflective compass was therefore essential if the patrol was to navigate safely and get back alive to its own trench before daybreak.

Artificial tree was an exact replica of the real tree it replaced

Soldier rests on internal step-ladder while looking through camouflaged peephole

German stereoscopic periscope

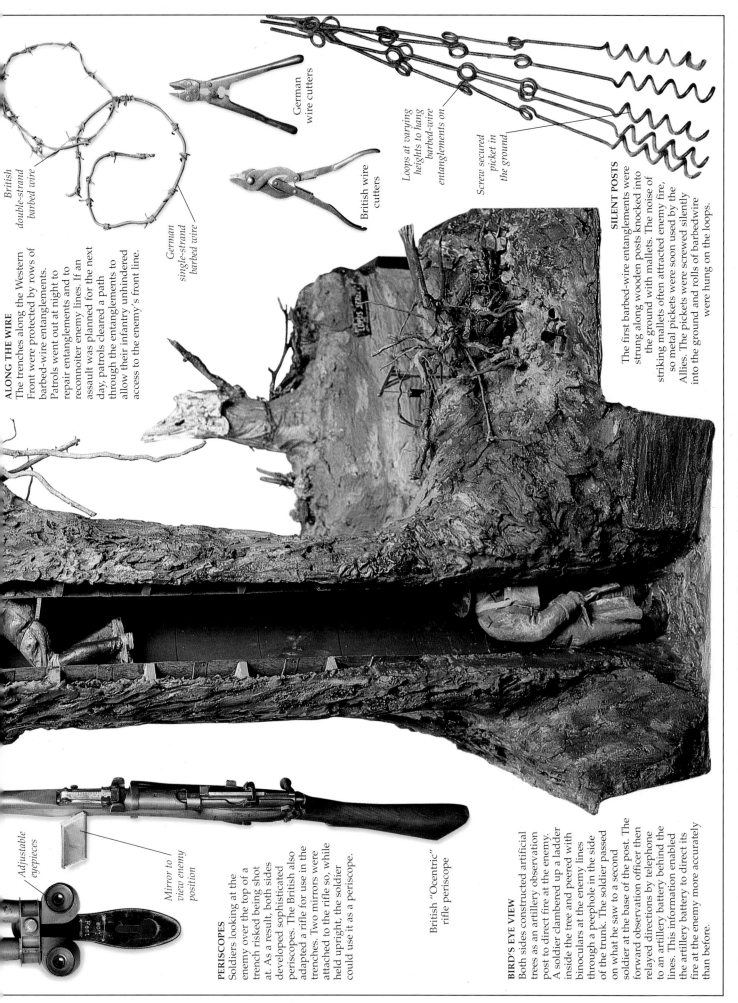

British double-strand barbed wire

German single-strand barbed wire

German wire cutters

British wire cutters

Loops at varying heights to hang barbed-wire entanglements on

Screw secured picket in the ground

ALONG THE WIRE

The trenches along the Western Front were protected by rows of barbed-wire entanglements. Patrols went out at night to repair entanglements and to reconnoiter enemy lines. If an assault was planned for the next day, patrols cleared a path through the entanglements to allow their infantry unhindered access to the enemy's front line.

SILENT POSTS

The first barbed-wire entanglements were strung along wooden posts knocked into the ground with mallets. The noise of striking mallets often attracted enemy fire, so metal pickets were soon used by the Allies. The pickets were screwed silently into the ground and rolls of barbedwire were hung on the loops.

Adjustable eyepieces

Mirror to view enemy position

PERISCOPES

Soldiers looking at the enemy over the top of a trench risked being shot at. As a result, both sides developed sophisticated periscopes. The British also adapted a rifle for use in the trenches. Two mirrors were attached to the rifle so, while held upright, the soldier could use it as a periscope.

British "Ocentric" rifle periscope

BIRD'S EYE VIEW

Both sides constructed artificial trees as an artillery observation post to direct fire at the enemy. A soldier clambered up a ladder inside the tree and peered with binoculars at the enemy lines through a peephole in the side of the trunk. The soldier passed on what he saw to a second soldier at the base of the post. The forward observation officer then relayed directions by telephone to an artillery battery behind the lines. This information enabled the artillery battery to direct its fire at the enemy more accurately than before.

Bombardment

SIGHT SAVER
In 1916–17 a chain-mail visor was added to the basic British helmet to protect the eyes. Visors were soon removed as they were difficult to see through.

BEWARE!
Soldiers at the front needed constant reminders to keep their heads down as they were so used to shells flying past. Warning signs were common.

Aʀᴛɪʟʟᴇʀʏ ᴅᴏᴍɪɴᴀᴛᴇᴅ the battlefields of World War I. A well-aimed bombardment could destroy enemy trenches, and knock out artillery batteries and communication lines. It could also help break up an infantry attack. But as defensive positions strengthened, artillery bombardments became longer and more intense. New tactics were required to break down enemy lines. The most effective was the creeping barrage, which rained down a moving curtain of heavy and insistent fire just ahead of attacking infantry.

Helmet

Visor for extra protection

GERMAN ARMOR
In January 1916 the German army replaced its distinctive spiked *Pickelhaube* with a rounded steel helmet. Body armor was first issued in 1916 to machine gunners.

Breastplate

Articulated plates to cover lower body

HIDING THE GUN
Two main types of artillery were used during the war – light field artillery, pulled by horses, and heavier guns, such as howitzers, moved by tractor and set up on reinforced beds. Once in place, artillery pieces were camouflaged to stop the enemy from destroying them.

British 8-in (20-cm) Mark V howitzer

SHELL POWER
The huge number of shells needed to maintain a constant artillery barrage against the enemy can be seen in this photograph of a British shell dump behind the Western Front.

LOADING A HOWITZER
Large pieces of artillery required a team of experienced gunners to load and fire them. This British 15-in (38-cm) howitzer was used on the Menin Road near Ypres, Belgium, in October 1917. The huge shell on the left of the picture is too large and heavy to lift, so is being winched into position.

EXPLOSION!
The devasting impact of artillery fire can be seen in this dramatic picture of a British tank hit by a shell and bursting into flames. To its right, another tank breaks through the barbed wire. It was unusual for moving targets, such as tanks, to be hit, and most artillery fire was used to soften up the enemy lines before an attack.

British 13-pounder (5.9-kg) high-explosive shell

French 75-mm (2.9-in) shrapnel shell

Fired from a howitzer

British 4.5 in- (11.4-cm) high-explosive shell

German 15-cm (5.9-in) shrapnel shell

CLASSIFYING SHELLS
Shells were classified by weight or diameter. High-explosive shells exploded on impact. Antipersonnel shrapnel shells exploded in flight and were designed to kill or maim.

Over the top

ONCE THE ARTILLERY bombardment had pounded the enemy's defenses, the infantry climbed out of the trenches and advanced toward enemy lines. The advance was very dangerous. Artillery bombardments rarely knocked out every enemy defense. Often, many gun emplacements and barbed-wire fences were still intact. Gaps in the defensive line were filled by highly mobile machine gunners. Against them, a soldier armed with only a rifle and bayonet and laden with heavy equipment was an easy target. On the first day of the Battle of the Somme in July 1916, German machine-gun fire accounted for two British soldiers killed or injured along each three feet (meter) of the 16-mile (28-km) front.

Steel water jacket to cool gun barrel

German MG '08 Maxim machine gun

Disc is part of the flash hider assembly, making the gun harder to spot

LEAVING THE TRENCH
The most frightening moment for a soldier was scrambling up a ladder out of his trench and into no-man's-land. Few men knew the horrors that awaited them.

Trench mounting

British .303 inch Maxim Mark 3 medium machine gun

Water-cooled barrel

Tripod mounting

QUICK FIRING
Machine guns fired up to 600 bullets a minute. Ammunition was put into a fabric or metal-link belt, or in a metal tray fed into the gun automatically. The gun barrel was surrounded with a cold-water jacket to cool it.

IN ACTION
This German machine-gun crew is protecting the flank (side) of an advancing infantry troop on the Western Front. The reliability and firepower of machine guns made them effective weapons. Also, their small size and maneuverability made them difficult for the enemy to destroy.

FUTILE ATTACK

The Battle of the Somme lasted from July 1, 1916, until November, 18, when snowstorms and rain brought the attack to a muddy halt. The Allies captured about 48 sq miles (125 sq km) of land, but failed to break through the German lines, reducing much of the area to a desolate wasteland. The Germans had been on the Somme since 1914, so knew the terrain well. The British belonged to Kitchener's new army. Young and inexperienced, this was the first battle many of them had fought in.

"The sunken road ... (was) ... filled with pieces of uniform, weapons, and dead bodies."

LIEUTENANT ERNST JUNGER, GERMAN SOLDIER, THE SOMME, 1916

First day on the Somme

The Allies planned to break through the German lines north of the Somme River, France, in 1916. On June, 24 the British began a six-day artillery bombardment on German lines, but the Germans retreated into deep bunkers and were largely unharmed. As the British infantry advanced at 7:30 am on July, 1 German machine gunners emerged from their bunkers and opened fire. Believing the artillery bombardment had destroyed German lines, the infantry marched in long, slow waves toward the enemy who literally mowed them down.

Below: Soldiers of the 103rd (Tyneside Irish) Brigade attack La Boisselle on the first day of the Somme

TENDING THE WOUNDED

The cramped conditions in a trench can be seen in this picture of an army medical officer tending a wounded soldier at Thiepval near the Somme in September 1916. Movement along a trench was often difficult and slow.

Casualty

No one knows how many soldiers were wounded in the war, but a likely estimate is 21 million. Caring for casualties was a major military operation. They were first treated at regimental aid posts in the trenches. Then, they were taken to casualty clearing stations behind the front line. Here, they received proper medical attention and basic surgery, if required, before being transported to base hospitals still farther from the front. Soldiers with severe injuries went home to recover in convalescent hospitals. Over 78% of British soldiers on the Western Front returned to active service. Illness was a major cause of casualty – in Mesopotamia over 50% of deaths were due to illness.

LUCKY MAN
Despite a fragment from a shell piercing his helmet, this soldier escaped with only a minor head wound. Many soldiers were not so fortunate, receiving severe injuries that stayed with them for life – if they survived at all.

Inventory listing contents and where to find them in the pouch

Bottles of liquid antiseptics and pain-killers

THE GERMAN KIT
German *Sanitätsmannschaften* (medical orderlies) carried two first-aid pouches on their belts. The pouch on the right (above) contained basic antiseptics, painkillers, and other treatments, while the pouch on the left contained dressings and triangular bandages.

TRENCH AID
Injured soldiers had their wounds dressed by medical orderlies in the trenches where they fell. They were then transferred to the regimental aid post, where their injuries could be assessed.

Strip of lace curtain

RECYCLED BANDAGES
Following the naval blockade by Britain, Germany ran out of cotton and linen. Wood fiber, paper, and lace curtains were used to make bandages instead.

German bandages

TOOLS OF THE TRADE
Army doctors carried a standard set of surgical instruments, as in this set issued by the Indian army. Their skills were in great demand, as they faced a wide variety of injuries from bullets and shell fragments that required immediate attention.

Forceps and clamps held securely in a metal tray

Lower tray contains saws and knives for amputation

THE FIELD HOSPITAL
Farmhouses, ruined factories, and even bombed-out churches, such as this one in Meuse, France, were used as casualty clearing stations to treat the wounded. Care was basic, and many were left to help themselves.

Shellshock

Shellshock is the collective name that was used to describe concussion, emotional shock, nervous exhaustion, and other similar ailments. Shellshock was not known before World War I, but trench warfare was so horrific that many soldiers developed shellshock during this war. Most of them eventually recovered, but some suffered nightmares and other symptoms for the rest of their lives. The illness caused a lot of controversy, and in 1922, the British War Office Committee said that shellshock did not exist and that it was a collection of already known illnesses.

A medical orderly helps a wounded soldier away from the trenches

Bunks for the injured to lie on

AMBULANCE
The British Royal Army Medical Corps, like its German counterpart, had a fleet of field ambulances to carry the wounded to the hospital. Many of these ambulances were staffed by volunteers, often women, and those from noncombatant countries such as the US.

Red Cross symbol to signify non-combatant status of the ambulance

Women at war

WHEN THE MEN went off to fight, the women were called upon to take their place on the homefront. Many women were already working, but their role was restricted to domestic labor, nursing, teaching, agricultural work on the family farm, and a few other jobs considered suitable for women. Now they went to work in factories, drove trucks and ambulances, and did almost everything that only men had done before. Many working women left their low-paid, low-status jobs for higher-paid work in munitions and other industries, achieving a new status in the eyes of society. Such gains, however, were short-lived, as most women returned to the home when the war ended.

ARMY LAUNDRY
Traditional prewar women's work, such as working in a laundry or bakery, continued during the war on a much larger scale. The French women employed at this British Army laundry in Prevent, France, in 1918 were washing and cleaning the dirty clothes of many thousands of soldiers every day.

FRONT-LINE ADVENTURE
For some women, the war was a big adventure. English nurse Elsie Knocker (above) went to Belgium in 1914 where she was joined by Scottish Mairi Chisholm. The women set up a dressing station at Pervyse, Belgium, and dressed the wounded until both were gassed in 1918. They were almost the only women on the front line. The two became known as the Women of Pervyse and were awarded the Order of Leopold by Belgian King Albert, and the British Military Medal. Elsie later married a Belgian officer, Baron de T'Sercles.

QUEEN MARY'S AUXILIARY
Few women actually fought in the war, but many were enlisted into auxiliary armies so that men could be released to fight on the front line. They drove trucks, repaired engines, and did much of the necessary administration and supply work. In Britain, many women joined The Women's (later Queen Mary's) Army Auxiliary Corps, whose recruiting poster featured a khaki-clad woman (left) with the words "The girl behind the man behind the gun." The women remained civilians, despite their military work.

WOMEN'S LAND ARMY

The war required a huge increase in food production at home as both sides tried to restrict the enemy's imports of food from abroad. In Britain, 113,000 women joined the Women's Land Army, set up in February 1917 to provide a well-paid female workforce to run the farms. Many members of the Land Army, such as this group of women, came from the middle and upper classes. They made a valuable contribution, but their numbers were insignificant compared with the millions of poorer women already employed on the land in the rest of Europe.

SUPPORT YOUR COUNTRY

Images of "ideal" women were used to gain support for a country's war effort. This Russian poster urges people to buy war bonds (fund-raising loans to the government) by linking Russian women to the love of the motherland.

RUSSIA'S AMAZONS

A number of Russian women joined the "Legion of Death" to fight for their country. The first battalion from Petrograd (St. Petersburg) distinguished itself by taking more than 100 German prisoners during a Russian retreat, although many of the women died in the battle.

Letters to men at the front describing events at home

Family photographs

Lace handkerchief

WORKING IN POVERTY

The war brought increased status and wealth to many women, but this was not the case everywhere. These Italian women worked in terrible conditions in a munitions factory. Many were very young and could not even afford shoes. This was common in factories across Italy, Germany, and Russia. The women worked long, hard hours but earned barely enough to feed their families. Strikes led by women were very common as a result.

MEMENTOS FROM HOME

Women kept in contact with their absent husbands, brothers, and sons by writing letters to them at the front. They also enclosed keepsakes of home, such as photographs or pressed flowers, to reassure the men that all was well in their absence and to remind them of home. Such letters and mementos did much to keep up the morale of homesick, and often very frightened, men.

War in the air

DOGFIGHTS
Pilots engaged in dogfights with enemy aircraft above the Western Front. Guns were mounted on top of the craft, so pilots had to fly straight at the enemy to shoot.

WHEN WAR BROKE OUT in August 1914, the history of powered flight was barely 10 years old. Aircraft had fought briefly in the Italian–Turkish war of 1911, but early aircraft development had been almost entirely for civilian use. Some military leaders could not even see how aircraft could be used in war, but they soon changed their minds. The first warplanes flew as reconnaissance craft, looking down on enemy lines or helping to direct artillery fire with great precision. Enemy pilots tried to shoot them down, leading to dogfights in the sky between highly skilled and immensely brave "aces." Specialized fighter planes, such as the Sopwith Camel and the German Fokker line, were soon produced by both sides, as were sturdier craft capable of carrying bombs to drop on enemy targets.

By the end of the war, the role of military aircraft had changed from being a minor help to the ground forces into a major force in their own right.

Leather face mask

Leather balaclava

Anti-splinter glass goggles

Raised collar to keep neck warm

Pouch to keep maps in

Coat of soft, supple leather

SOPWITH CAMEL
The Sopwith F1 Camel first flew in battle in June 1917 and became the most successful Allied fighter in shooting down German aircraft. Pilots enjoyed flying the Camel because of its exceptional agility and ability to make sharp turns at high speed.

Wooden box-structure wings covered with canvas

Sheepskin-lined leather gloves to protect against frostbite

26-ft 11-in (8.2-m) wingspan

Propeller to guide the bomb

BOMBS AWAY
The first bombs were literally dropped over the side of the aircraft by the pilot. Specialized bomber aircraft soon appeared, equipped with bombsights, bomb racks beneath the fuselage, and release systems operated by the pilot or another crew member.

DRESSED FOR THE AIR
Pilots flew in open cockpits, so they wore soft leather coats and balaclavas, sheepskin-lined fur boots, and sheepskin-lined leather gloves to keep out the cold. Later in the war, one-piece suits of waxed cotton lined with silk and fur became common.

Sheepskin boots

Thick sole to give a good grip

British 20-lb (9.1-kg) Marten Hale bomb, containing 4.5 lb (2 kg) of explosives

Fins to stop the bomb from spinning on its descent

Perforated casing to help bomb catch fire on impact

British Carcass incendiary bomb

Fokker DV11

Side cutaway to show internal steel-tubing framework

GERMAN FIGHTER
The formidable German Fokker DVII appeared in April 1918. Although slower than the Sopwith Camel, it climbed rapidly, recovered quickly from a dive, and flew well at all altitudes.

BMW engine

Wooden struts

N6812

Symbol of British Royal Flying Corps, later the Royal Air Force

MANEUVERS
The art of aerial warfare was unknown to pilots at the start of the war and had to be learned from scratch. This British instruction poster shows the correct method of attacking a German fighter, although theory on the ground was no substitute for actual experience in the sky.

German aircraft holds a steady course

British fighter comes up from below and behind

> "You ask me to 'let the devils have it'... when I fight ... I don't think them devils ... I only scrap because it is my duty."
>
> CAPTAIN ALBERT BALL, 1916

Barrel could fire 1-pound shell

Pivot to change direction and angle of gun

Captain René Fonck (France) – 75 hits (1894–1953)

Captain Albert Ball (Britain) – 44 hits (1896–1917)

Rittmeister Manfred von Richthofen (Germany), center – 80 hits (1892–1918)

AIR ACES
To qualify as an air "ace," a pilot had to bring down at least 10 enemy aircraft. Those who did became national heroes. Baron von Richthofen – the "Red Baron" – was the highest-scoring ace of the war, shooting down 80 Allied aircraft. The British ace, Captain Albert Ball, had more decorations for bravery than any other man of his age, including the Victoria Cross; he was only 20 when he was shot down and killed in 1917.

Captain Eddie Rickenbacker (USA) – 24 ⅓ hits (1890–1973)

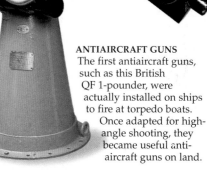

ANTIAIRCRAFT GUNS
The first antiaircraft guns, such as this British QF 1-pounder, were actually installed on ships to fire at torpedo boats. Once adapted for high-angle shooting, they became useful anti-aircraft guns on land.

Zeppelin

IN THE SPRING OF 1915, the first German airships appeared in Britain's night sky. The sight of these huge, slow-moving machines caused enormous panic – at any moment a hail of bombs could fall from the airship. Yet in reality, airships played little part in the war. The first airship was designed by a German, Count Ferdinand von Zeppelin in 1900. Airships are often called zeppelins, but technically only those designed by him should bear the name. Early in the war, airships could fly higher than planes, so it was almost impossible to shoot them down. This made them useful for bombing raids. But soon, higher-flying aircraft and the use of incendiary (fire-making) bullets brought these aerial bombers down to earth. By 1917, most German and British airships were restricted to reconnaissance work at sea.

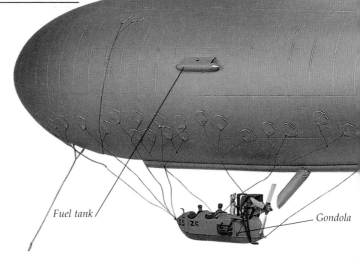

Fuel tank

Gondola

INSIDE THE GONDOLA
The crew operated the airship from the gondola – a spacious cabin below the main airship. The gondola had open sides, so the crew had little protection from the weather.

BOMBS AWAY!
Crews in the first airships had to drops their bombs, such as this incendiary bomb, over the side of the gondola by hand. Later models had automatic release mechanisms.

German incendiary bomb dropped by Zeppelin LZ38 on London, May 31, 1915

GETTING BIGGER
This L3 German airship took part in the first airship raid on Britain on the night of January 19–20, 1915, causing 20 civilian casualties. Eyewitnesses were scared by its size, but by 1918 Germany was producing ships almost three times as big.

Stabilizer

Emblem of British Royal Naval Air Service

SEA SCOUT ZERO
The British SSZ (Sea Scout Zero) was first put into service in 1916. It was a nonrigid airship, meaning it had no internal framework. Its light weight gave it an impressive top speed of 45 mph (72 km/h), and it could stay airborne for 17 hours. Its crew of three was employed mainly on submarine patrol or on escort duty for convoys.

Observer

Engine and propeller to provide power and steer airship

The engine gantry was linked to the gondola by a rope ladder

Gantry

Float in case airship landed on sea

Lewis gunner

HIGH ABOVE THE SEAS
The British used airships mainly to patrol the seas looking for German U-boats. The machine gunner protected the crew and ship against an enemy fighter, while other crew members were on lookout. These two crew members are perching on a flimsy gantry mounted to the side of the gondola strung beneath the airship.

CAPITAL TARGET
The first German airship raid on London took place on May 31, 1915, and was followed by a more powerful attack on 8 September. The artist R. Schmidt from Hamburg recorded one such night raid. In total, there were 51 airship attacks on British cities. 196 tons of bombs were dropped, killing 557 people and wounding 1,358.

War at sea

SINCE THE LAUNCH OF Britain's Dreadnought battleship in 1906, Britain, Germany, and other countries had engaged in a massive naval building program. Yet the war itself was fought largely on land, and both sides avoided naval conflict. The British needed their fleet to keep the seas open for merchant ships bringing food and other supplies to Britain, as well as to prevent supplies from reaching Germany. Germany needed its fleet to protect itself against possible invasion. The only major sea battle – off Jutland in the North Sea in 1916 – was inconclusive. The main fight took place under the sea, as German U-boats waged a damaging war against Allied ships in an effort to force Britain out of the war.

"I WANT YOU"
When the US entered the war in April 1917, a poster showing an attractive woman in naval uniform (above) urged volunteers to enlist.

CONSTANT THREAT
This German propaganda poster, *The U-boats are out!*, shows the threat posed to Allied shipping by the German U-boat fleet.

LIFE INSIDE A U-BOAT
Conditions inside a U-boat were cramped and uncomfortable. Fumes and heat from the engine and poor ventilation made the air very stuffy. The crew had to navigate the craft through minefields and avoid detection from reconnaissance aircraft in order to attack enemy ships.

Floats for landing on water

LAND AND SEA
Seaplanes are able to take off and land on both water and ground. They were used for reconnaissance and bombing work. This version of the Short 184 was the first seaplane to sink an enemy ship with a torpedo.

Observation balloon

Gun

SUCCESS AND FAILURE
German U-boats operated both under the sea and on the surface. Here, the crew is opening fire with a deck cannon to stop an enemy steamer. German U-boats sank 5,554 Allied and neutral merchant ships as well as many warships. Their own losses, however, were also considerable. Out of a total fleet of 372 German U-boats, 178 were destroyed by Allied bombs or torpedoes.

CONFUSE AND SURVIVE

In 1917 the British Admiralty began to camouflage merchant ships with strange and garish designs. These gray, black, and blue geometric patterns distorted the silhouette of the ship and made it difficult for German U-boats to determine its course and thus aim torpedoes at it with any accuracy. More than 2,700 merchant ships and 400 convoy escorts were camouflaged in this way before the war ended.

DAZZLED

During the war, many artists contributed to their country's war effort some in surprising ways. The modern British painter Edward Wadsworth supervised the application of "dazzle" camouflage to ships' hulls. He later painted a picture (above), *Dazzle ships in dry dock at Liverpool*, of the finished result.

Medals awarded to Jack Cornwall

Victoria Cross (VC)   British War Medal   Victory Medal

BOY (1ST CLASS)

John Travers Cornwall was only 16 when he first saw action at the Battle of Jutland on May 31, 1916. He was a ship's boy (1st class) aboard HMS *Chester* and was mortally wounded early in the battle. While other crew members lay dead or injured, Cornwall stayed at his post until the end of the action. He died of his wounds on June 2, and was posthumously awarded the Victoria Cross.

THE BRITISH GRAND FLEET

The British Royal Navy was the biggest and most powerful in the world. It operated a policy known as the "two-power standard" – the combined might of the British fleet should be the equal of the two next strongest nations combined. Despite this superiority, the navy played a fairly minor role in the war compared to the army, keeping the seas free of German ships and escorting convoys of merchant ships to Britain.

Flight deck

HMS FURIOUS

Aircraft carriers first saw service during World War I. On July 7, 1918, seven Sopwith Camels took off from the deck of HMS *Furious* to attack the zeppelin base at Tondern in northern Germany, destroying both sheds and the two Zeppelins inside.

Gallipoli

TASTY GREETINGS
British army cookies were often easier to write on than to eat, as this hard-baked Christmas card from Gallipoli illustrates.

IN EARLY 1915, the Allies decided to force through the strategic, but heavily fortified, Dardanelles straits and capture the Ottoman Turkish capital of Constantinople. Naval attacks on February 19, and March 18 both failed. On April 25, British, Australian, and New Zealand troops landed on the Gallipoli peninsula, while French troops staged a diversion to their south. In August, there was a second landing at Suvla Bay, also on the peninsula. Although the landings were a success, the casualty rate was high and the Allies were unable to move far from the beaches due to fierce Turkish resistance. As the months wore on, the death rate mounted. The Allies eventually withdrew in January 1916, leaving the Ottoman Empire still in control of the Dardanelles and still in the war.

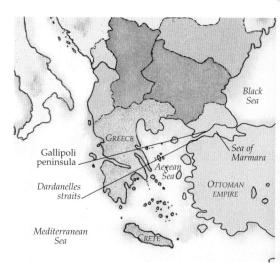

GALLIPOLI PENINSULA
The Gallipoli peninsula lies to the north of the Dardanelles, a narrow waterway connecting the Aegean Sea to the Black Sea via the Sea of Marmara. Control of this waterway would have given Britain and France a direct sea route from the Mediterranean to the Black Sea and their ally, Russia. But both sides of the waterway were controlled by Germany's ally, the Ottoman Empire.

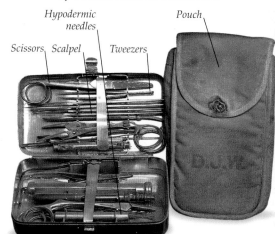

Privately purchased medical kit used by a British officer on the front line

Hypodermic needles — *Pouch* — *Scissors* — *Scalpel* — *Tweezers*

THE CASUALTY RATE
Despite the efforts of the medical staff, some of whom even carried portable surgical kits, the treatment and evacuation of casualties from Gallipoli was complicated by the enormous numbers of soldiers who were sick, as well as those who were wounded.

Jetty for boats carrying sick and wounded soldiers

THE SICK BEACH
Both sides had their food contaminated by flies carrying disease from the many corpses. Dysentery was endemic – in September 1915, 78% of the Anzac troops in the No. 1 Australian Stationary Hospital at Anzac Cove (above) were being treated for the disease.

GERMAN HELP
The Allies expected the Gallipoli peninsula to be lightly defended, but with the help of Germany, the Turks had built strong defensive positions. They dug trenches, erected barbed-wire fences, and built well-guarded artillery positions. Germany also equipped the Turks with modern pistols, rifles, and machine guns.

IMPROVISED GRENADES
The fighting at Gallipoli was often at very close range. Hand-thrown grenades were particularly effective in knocking out enemy positions. During a munitions shortage, Allied troops improvised by making grenades out of tin cans.

Narrow beach unprotected against Turkish fire

Turkish defenses look down on beach

KEMAL ATATURK
Born in 1881, Mustafa Kemal distinguished himself fighting for the Ottoman Turkish army in Libya in 1911 and against the Bulgarians in 1912–13. At Gallipoli, Kemal was appointed divisional commander, where he helped to strengthen the Ottoman Turkish defenses. Kemal then brilliantly led the 19th Division on the ridges above Anzac Cove, preventing the Allies from penetrating inland. After the war, Kemal led a revolt to prevent the dismemberment of Turkey. In 1923, he became the first president of the Turkish Republic until his death in 1938, later gaining the name Atatürk (Father of the Turks).

ANZAC COVE
On April 25, the Australian and New Zealand Army Corps, known as the Anzacs, landed on the western coast of the Gallipoli peninsula. All hopes of swiftly capturing the peninsula were thwarted by the unyielding terrain. The beach was very narrow and the steep, sandy hills gave the men no cover. They were under constant fire from the well-hidden Ottoman Turks above. The beach is now known as Anzac Cove as a sign of remembrance.

Sultan's Cypher with the year 1333 in the Muslim calendar, which is 1915 in the Western calendar

WINTER EVACUATION
On December 7, 1915, the Allies decided to withdraw from Gallipoli. A flotilla of ships evacuated the troops and their supplies. Unlike the chaos and carnage of the previous six months, the withdrawals under the cover of darkness went without a hitch and not a single person was injured. British and Anzac forces withdrew from Anzac and Suvla on the night of December 18–19, with the rest of the British forces at Cape Helles following on January 8–9, 1916.

FOR DISTINCTION
The Turkish Order of the Crescent was instituted on March 1, 1915 for distinguished service. It was awarded to German and Turkish soldiers who fought at Gallipoli.

Hyde Park Memorial, Sydney, Australia

ANZAC MEMORIAL
During the war, both Australia and New Zealand suffered large numbers of deaths in proportion to their small populations. Australia lost 60,000 men from a population of less than five million. New Zealand lost 17,000 from a population of one million. Of those, 11,100 died at Gallipoli. Today, Australia and New Zealand remember their war dead on Anzac Day, April 25.

Many soldiers were suffering from frostbite

Large horse-drawn gun

British soldiers evacuated by raft from Suvla Bay, December 19, 1915

The battle of Verdun

ON FEBRUARY 21, 1916, Germany launched a massive attack against Verdun, a fortified French city. Verdun lay close to the German border and controlled access into eastern France. After a huge, eight-hour artillery bombardment, the German infantry advanced. The French were caught by surprise and lost control of some of their main forts, but during the summer their resistance stiffened. By December, the Germans had been pushed back almost to where they started. The cost to both sides was enormous – over 400,000 French casualties and 336,831 German casualties. The German General Falkenhayn later claimed he had tried to bleed France to death. He did not succeed, and including losses at the Battle of the Somme, German casualties that year were 774,153.

BURNING WRECKAGE
On February 25, the ancient city of Verdun was evacuated. Many buildings were hit by the artillery bombardment, and even more destroyed by the fires that often raged for days. Firefighters did their best to control the blazes, but large numbers of houses had wooden frames and burned easily.

GENERAL PETAIN
General Henri-Philippe Pétain took command of the French forces of Verdun on February 25, the same day as the loss of Fort Douaumont. He organized an effective defense of the town and made sure the army was properly supplied. His rallying cry, "Ils ne passeront pas!" (They shall not pass!), did much to raise French morale.

Exposed concrete fort wall

Machine-gun post

Double-breasted overcoat

Horizon-blue uniform

Haversack

LE POILU
The French slang for an infantry soldier was *le poilu*, or "hairy one." *Les poilus* bore the brunt of the German attack, enduring the muddy, cold, and wet conditions and suffering appalling injuries from shellfire and poison gas.

FORT DOUAUMONT
Verdun was protected by three rings of fortifications. Fort Douaumont, in the outer ring, was the strongest of these forts. It was built of steel and concrete and surrounded by ramparts, ditches, and rolls of barbed wire. But although the fort itself was strong, it was defended by just 56 elderly reservists. The fort fell to the Germans on February 25.

Lebel rifle

Steel helmet

Thick boots with puttees wrapped around the legs

Background picture: ruined Verdun cityscape, 1916

AT CLOSE QUARTERS

Fighting at Verdun was particularly fierce, as both sides repeatedly attacked and counterattacked the same forts and strategic areas around the city. Advancing attackers were assaulted by hails of machine-gun fire from the enemy within the forts. The open ground was so exposed that it was impossible to retrieve the dead, and the corpses were left to rot in the ground. The forts were also riddled with underground tunnels where both sides engaged in vicious hand-to-hand combat. Many dramatic films have been made about the war, and this photograph comes from one such film.

> *"What a bloodbath, what horrid images, what a slaughter. I just cannot find the words to express my feelings. Hell cannot be this dreadful."*
>
> **ALBERT JOUBAIRE**
> FRENCH SOLDIER, VERDUN, 1916

URROUNDING VILLAGES

he village of Ornes was one of many rench villages attacked and captured uring the German advance on erdun. The devastation was so great at this village, along with eight thers, was not rebuilt after the war, ut is still marked on maps as a sign f remembrance.

Laurel-leaf wreath

Oak-leaf wreath

Head of Marianne,
symbol of France

LEGION D'HONNEUR

In recognition of the suffering experienced by Verdun's population, French president Raymond Poincaré varded the city the *Légion d'Honneur*. The honor is usually presented to men and women, military and civilian, for bravery.

THE MUDDY INFERNO

The countryside around Verdun is wooded and hilly, with many streams running down to the Meuse River. Heavy rainfall and constant artillery bombardment turned this landscape into a desolate mudbath, where the bodies of the dead lay half-buried in shell craters and men were forced to eat and sleep within inches of their fallen comrades. This photograph shows the "Ravine de la mort," the Ravine of the Dead.

Gas attack

Oɴ ᴛʜᴇ ᴀꜰᴛᴇʀɴᴏᴏɴ of April 22, 1915, French-Algerian troops near the Belgian town of Ypres noticed a greenish-yellow cloud moving toward them from the German front. The cloud was chlorine gas. This was the first time poison gas had been used effectively in war. As it reached the Allied line, many soldiers panicked, since they had no protection against its choking effects. Over the next three years, both sides used gas – the Germans released about 68,000 tons, the British and French 51,000 tons. The first gas clouds were released from canisters and blown by the wind toward the enemy, but this caused problems if the wind changed and blew the gas in the wrong direction. More effective were gas-filled shells, which could be targeted at enemy lines. In total, 1,200,000 soldiers on both sides were gassed, of whom 91,198 died terrible deaths.

British "Hypo" helmet

EARLY WARNING
The first anti-gas masks were crude and often ineffectual, as these instructional drawings from a British training school show. Basic goggles protected the eyes, while mouthpads made of flannel or other absorbent materials were worn over the mouth. Chemicals soaked into the pads neutralized the gas.

British anti-gas goggles

Black veil respirator

Flannel respirator

Air tube

Chemical filter to neutralize gas

Gas alarm whistle

ALL-IN-ONE
By the middle of the war, both sides wore fully protective helmets, which consisted of face masks, goggles, and respirators. These protected the eyes, nose, and throat from the potentially lethal effects of gas.

GASSED!
The full horror of being blinded by gas is caught in *Gassed*, a painting from real life by the American artist John Singer Sargent. Led by their sighted colleagues, the blinded soldiers are slowly shuffling toward a dressing station near Arras in northern France in August 1918.

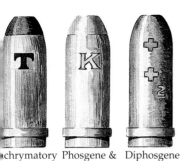

GAS SHELLS

Gas shells contained liquid gas, which evaporated on impact. Gases caused a range of injuries depending on their type. Gases such as chlorine, diphosgene, and phosgene caused severe breathing difficulties, while benzyl bromide caused the eyes to water. Dichlorethylsulphide burned and blistered the skin, caused temporary blindness and, if inhaled, flooded the lungs and led to death from pneumonia.

chrymatory   Phosgene &   Diphosgene   Diphosgene   Mustard
             Diphosgene   & Sneezing   Oil
                          Oil

Glove shrunken by gas

Ordinary glove

UNDER ATTACK

The first effects of gas were felt on the face and in the eyes, but within seconds it entered the throat. Soldiers coughed and choked as the gas swirled around them. The long-term effects depended on the type of gas used – some soldiers died very quickly, others were blinded for life or suffered awful skin blisters, while some died a lingering death as their lungs collapsed and filled with liquid. The only protection was to wear combined goggles and respirator. Major Tracy Evert photographed these American soldiers in 1918. They are posing to illustrate the ill effects of forgetting their gas masks. The photograph was used when training new recruits.

HAND SHRUNK

When exposed to some kinds of gas, a glove like the one above will shrink to the size of the glove above, right. This is what happens to a person's lungs when exposed to the same gas.

German gas mask

Eyes not protected

Canvas-covered respirator

ANIMAL WELFARE

Every living creature was vulnerable to gas, including the many thousands of horses used by both sides to transport men, equipment, and supplies. Here, both German rider and horse have got their gas masks on, although the horse's eyes remain unprotected and vulnerable.

The Eastern Front

WHEN PEOPLE TODAY think of World War I, they picture the fighting in the trenches along the Western Front. But on the other side of Europe, a very different war took place, between Germany and Austria-Hungary on one side and Russia on the other. This war was much more fluid, with great armies marching backward and forward across many hundreds of miles. Both the Austro-Hungarian and Russian armies were badly led and poorly equipped, and both suffered huge losses. In 1915 alone, the Russians lost two million men, of whom one million were taken prisoner. The German army, ably led by General Hindenburg, was far more effective. By the end of 1916, despite some Russian successes, the Germans were in full control of the entire Eastern Front. The Russians were greatly demoralized and this led, in part, to the Russian Revolution the following year, 1917.

TANNENBERG, 1914
In August 1914, Russia's First and Second armies invaded East Prussia, Germany. The Russians did not disguise their messages in code, so the Germans knew what to expect. The Second Army was soon surrounded at Tannenberg and was forced to surrender on August 31, with the loss of 150,000 men and all of its artillery (above).

MASURIAN LAKES, 1914
In September 1914, the Russian First Arm was by the Masurian Lakes in East Pruss It was in danger of being surrounded as the Second Army had been the previous month at Tannenberg. German troops du trenches and other defenses (above) and attacked the Russians, who soon withdre sustaining more than 100,000 casualties. the end of September, the Russian threat Germany was over.

INITIAL SUCCESS
During 1914, the Russian army conquered Austria-Hungary's eastern province of Galicia, inflicting huge defeats on the Austro-Hungarian army. But, in 1915, German reinforcements (above) pushed the Russians back into their own country.

UNWILLING TO FIGHT
By the end of 1916, many Russian soldiers were refusing to fight. They were badly treated, ill-equipped, poorly led, and starving. They saw little reason to risk their lives in a war they did not believe in. Officers had to threaten their troops to make them fight, and mutinies were common, although many thousands simply deserted and went home.

The Italian Front

On May 23, 1915, Italy joined the war on the side of the Allies and prepared to invade its hostile neighbor, Austria-Hungary. Fighting took place on two fronts – north and east. Italy fought against the Italian-speaking Trentino region of Austria-Hungary to the north, and along the Isonzo River to the east. The Italian army was ill-prepared and underequipped for the war, and was unable to break through the Austrian defenses until its final success at the Battle of Vittorio-Veneto in October 1918.

THE ISONZO
The Isonzo River formed a natural boundary between the mountains of Austria-Hungary and the plains of northern Italy. Between June 1915 and August 1917, the two sides fought 11 inconclusive battles along the river before the Austrians, with German support, achieved a decisive victory at Caporetto in December 1917.

ITALIAN ALPINISTS
All but 20 miles (32 km) of the 400-mile (640-km) Italian frontier with Austria-Hungary lay in the Italian Alps. Both sides used trained alpine troops to fight in mountainous terrain. Every mountain peak became a potential observation post or gun emplacement.

Russian troops marching to defend the newly captured city of Przemysl in Austrian Galicia

War in the desert

FIGHTING DURING World War I was not restricted just to Europe. German colonies in Africa were overrun by French, British, and South African forces, while Germany's colonies in China and the Pacific were overrun by Japanese, British, Australian, and New Zealand forces. One of the major conflicts took place in the Middle East. Here, the Turkish Ottoman Empire controlled Mesopotamia (modern Iraq), Palestine, Syria, and Arabia. British and Indian troops invaded Mesopotamia in 1914 and finally captured Baghdad in 1917. Meanwhile, a large British force, under General Allenby, captured Palestine and, in the last weeks of the war, the Syrian capital of Damascus. In Arabia, Bedouin soldiers under the guidance of T.E. Lawrence rose in revolt against their Turkish rulers and waged a guerrilla campaign for an independent Arab state.

SPINE PAD
The British army was concerned that soldiers fighting in the desert might get heatstroke. They therefore issued spine pads to protect the soldiers' backs from the sun. The weight and discomfort of the pad would have done little to keep the body cool.

Arab flintlock pistol

Lawrence's rifle

Lawrence's initials

RETURN JOURNEY
British soldier T. E. Lawrence's rifle was one of the many British rifles captured by the Turks at Gallipoli in 1915. It was then given by the Turkish War Minister, Enver Pasha, to the Arab leader, Emir Feisal, who in turn presented it to Lawrence in December 1916.

LAWRENCE OF ARABIA
The British soldier T. E. Lawrence is a romantic, almost legendary figure known as Lawrence of Arabia. Lawrence first visited the Middle East in 1909, and learned to speak Arabic. In 1914, he became an army intelligence officer in Cairo, Egypt. Later, he worked as liaison officer to Emir Feisal, leader of the Arab revolt against Ottoman Turkish rule. Lawrence helped the Arabs to become an effective guerrilla force, blowing up railroad lines, attacking Turkish garrisons, and tying down an army many times their own size.

JERICHO RD
TO DAMASCUS GTE
& NABLUS ROAD.
TO JAFFA GTE
STATION &
HEBRON RD

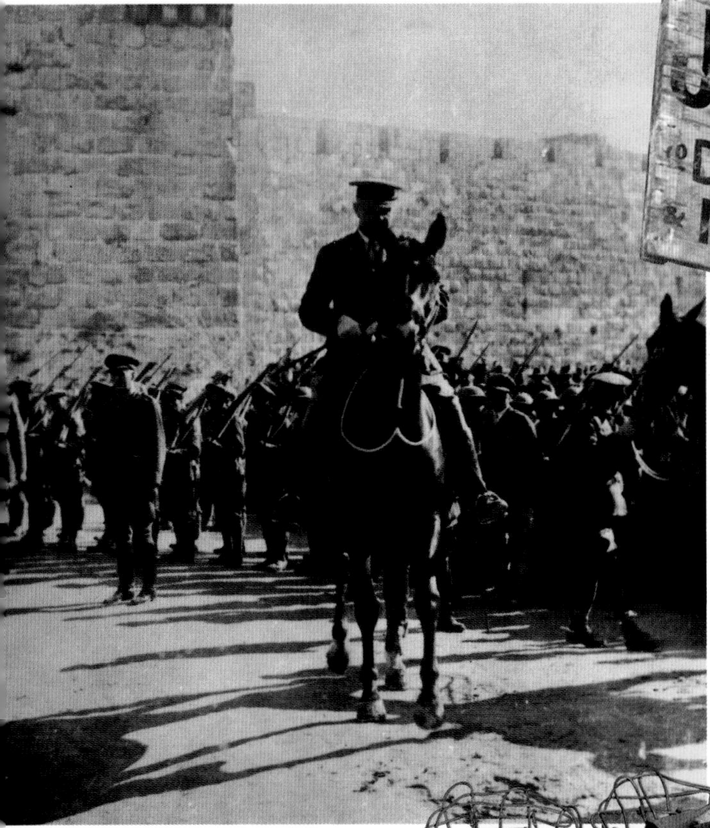

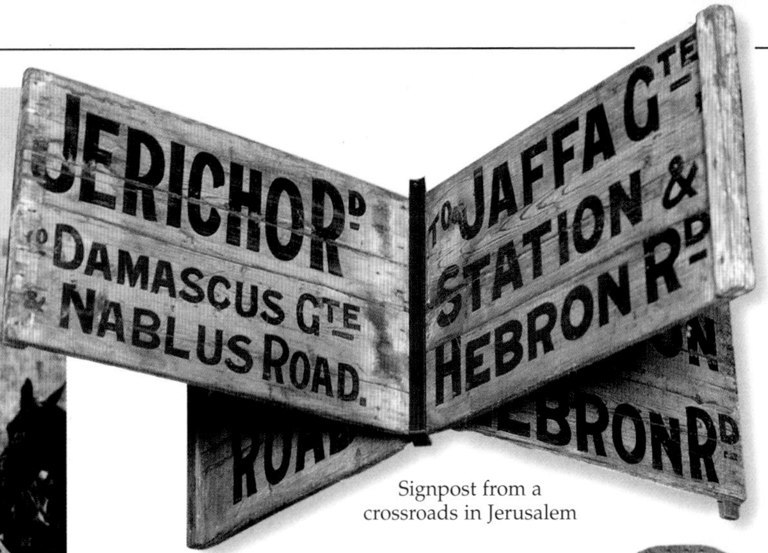

Signpost from a crossroads in Jerusalem

FIGHTING IN PALESTINE
In early 1917, Britain opened a new front against Ottoman Turkey. British troops invaded Palestine, and, after early failures, General Allenby captured and entered Jerusalem on December 11, 1917 (left). After a pause, fighting resumed in the fall of 1918. British troops pushed north toward Damascus, while an Arab army under Lawrence continued to attack the Turks in the desert. Both armies entered Damascus on October 1, 1918. Within a month, Ottoman Turkey had surrendered.

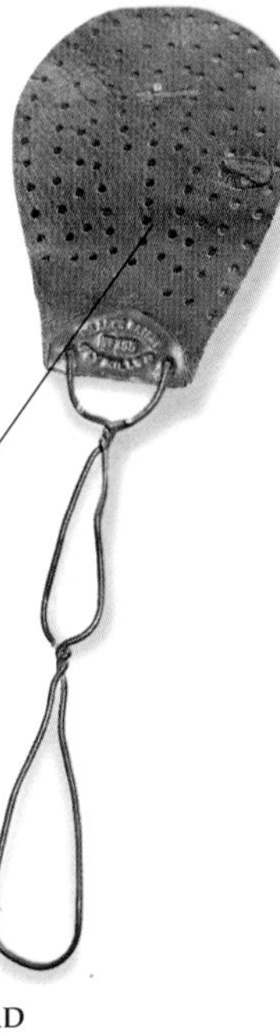

Swatter made of perforated, flexible leather
Wire strap

FLY SWATTER
The British army made sure its personnel were issued with every necessity for desert warfare, including fly swatters!

Leather loop
Webbing strap

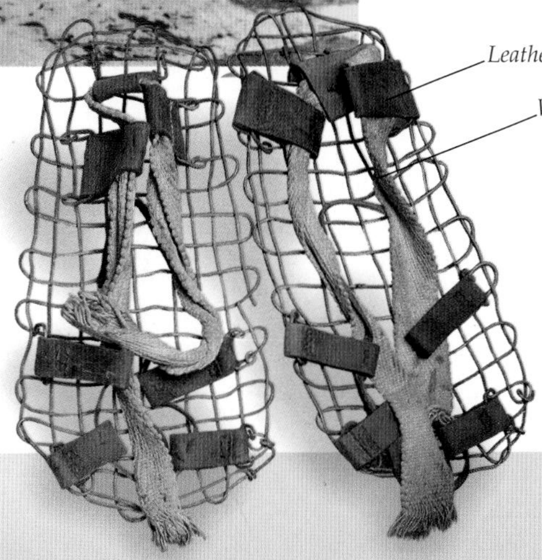

SAND SHOES
Walking across soft, shifting sand in egular army boots was very tiring. These British wire sand shoes were worn over the boot and tied in place with webbing straps. They helped spread the soldier's weight, so he did not sink in the sand.

MARCH TO BAGHDAD
Turkish-held Mesopotamia was rich in oil, which Britain needed to supply its navy with fuel. In November 1914, Britain sent troops to protect its interests in the oil fields of Basra in Mesopotamia. The commander, General Townsend then decided to advance up the Tigris River toward Baghdad. But his men were ill-prepared for a long campaign, and in April 1916 their garrison at Kut al-Amarah was forced to surrender to Turkish troops, seen here crossing a pontoon bridge in Baghdad. The British finally captured Baghdad in March 1917.

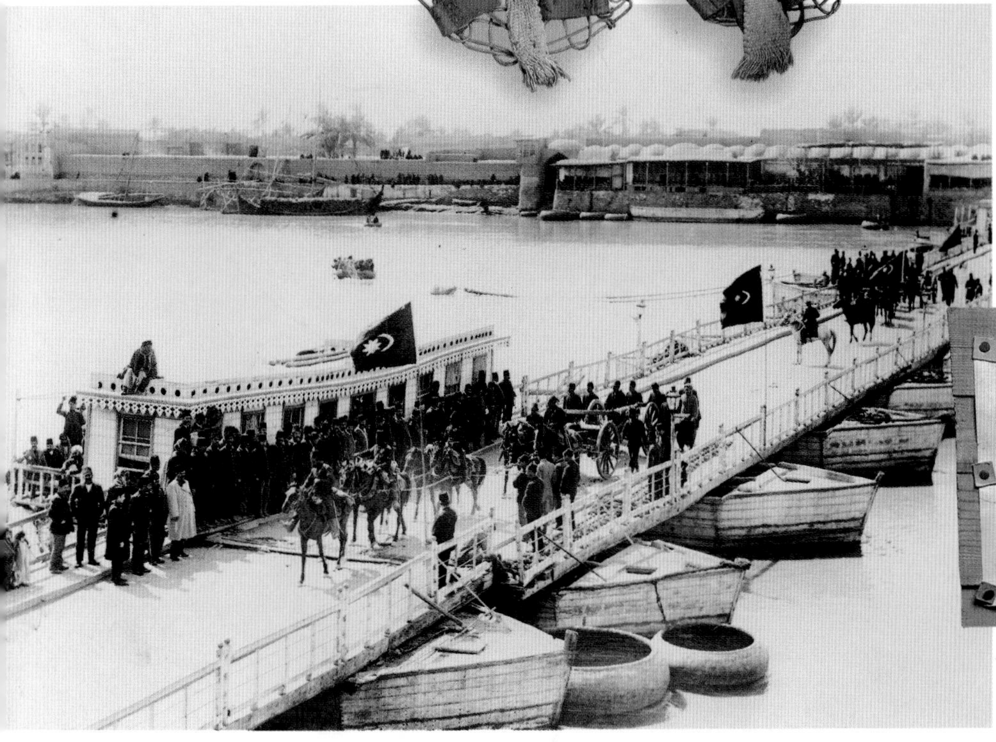

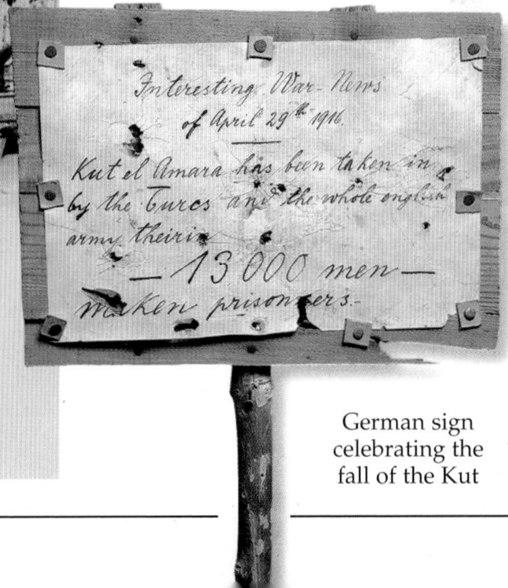

Interesting War-News
of April 29th 1916.
Kut el Amara has been taken in by the Turcs and the whole english army theirin
— 13 000 men —
maken prisoners.

German sign celebrating the fall of the Kut

Espionage

BOTH SIDES SUSPECTED the other of employing hundreds of spies to report on enemy intentions and capabilities. In fact, most espionage work consisted not of spying on enemy territory but of eavesdropping on enemy communications. Code-breaking or cryptography was very important as both sides sent and received coded messages by radio and telegraph. Cryptographers devised highly complex codes to ensure the safe transit of their own messages while using their skills to intercept and break coded enemy messages. Such skills enabled British intelligence to decipher the Zimmermann telegram from Berlin to Washington sent in January 1917, leading to the entry of the US into the war in April 1917.

Lightweight, but strong, string attaches parachute to bird

Corselet made of linen and padded to protect bird

POSTAL PIGEON
Over 500,000 pigeons were used during the war to carry messages between intelligence agents and their home bases. The pigeons were dropped by parachute into occupied areas. Agents collected the pigeons at drop zones and looked after them until they had information to send home. When released, the birds flew home to their lofts with messages attached to their legs.

EDITH CAVELL
Edith Cavell was born in England and worked as a governess in Belgium in the early 1890s before training in England as a nurse. In 1907 she returned to Belgium to start a nursing school in Brussels (above). When the Germans occupied the city in August 1914 she decided to stay, accommodating up to 200 British soldiers who also found themselves behind enemy lines. The Germans arrested her and tried her for "conducting soldiers to the enemy." She was found guilty and executed by firing squad in October 1915. Cavell was not a spy, but her execution did provide a powerful propaganda weapon for the Allies.

IN MINIATURE
Pigeons could not carry much weight, so messages had to be written on small pieces of paper. This message, in German, is written on a standard "pigeon post" form used by the German army. Long messages could be photographed with a special camera that reduced them to the size of a microdot – that is 300 hundred times smaller than the original.

Front of button

Coded message on back of button

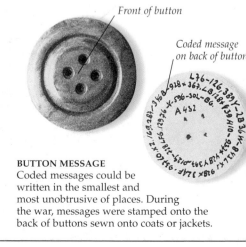

SECRET INK
Invisible ink was used to conceal messages written on paper. The invisible message could be read later when the paper was treated with a chemical to make the words visible.

German invisible ink and sponge

Invisible ink bottle

BUTTON MESSAGE
Coded messages could be written in the smallest and most unobtrusive of places. During the war, messages were stamped onto the back of buttons sewn onto coats or jackets.

POCKET CAMERA

Lens cap

Camera lens

Small cameras hidden in a pocket or disguised as a pocket watch were used to take clandestine photographs. This spy camera was used in German East Africa (now Tanzania).

Shutter release

READING THE ENEMY

Army intelligence officers, such as this British soldier, played a vital role in examining and understanding captured enemy documents. Painstaking reading of every piece of information enabled the intelligence services to build up a reasonably complete picture about enemy preparations for an attack. They could also assess the state of civilian morale, and pass that information on to the military high command.

HIDDEN MESSAGES

Not every spy remained undetected. Two agents from the Netherlands sent to Portsmouth, England, to spy for Germany pretended to be cigar importers. They used their orders for imported Dutch cigars as codes for the ships they observed in Portsmouth harbor. They were caught and executed in 1915.

Cigars slit open in search of hidden messages

AID TO ESCAPE

This can, supposedly containing ox tongue, was sent to British Lieutenant Jack Shaw at the German prisoner of war camp, Holzminden in 1918. It contained maps, wire cutters, and compasses to help Shaw arrange a mass escape from the camp.

Rolled-up map of France

Lead weights to make the can the correct weight

Compass

MATA HARI

Dutch-born Margaretta Zelle was a famous dancer who used the stage-name Mata Hari. She had many high-ranking lovers, which enabled her to pass on any confidential information she acquired from them to the secret services. In 1914, while dancing in Paris, she was recruited by the French intelligence service. She went to Madrid, where she tried to win over a German diplomat. He double-crossed her with false information, and on her return to France she was arrested, tried, and found guilty of being a German agent. She was executed by firing squad in October 1917.

Tank warfare

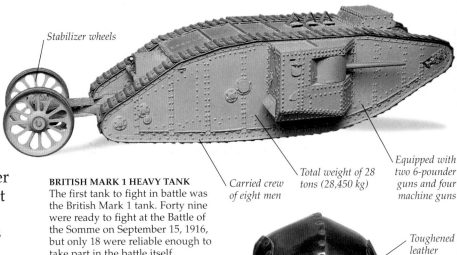

Stabilizer wheels

THE BRITISH-INVENTED tank was a major mechanical innovation of the war. British tanks first saw action in 1916, but these early tanks were not very reliable. It was not until November 1917, at the Battle of Cambrai, that their full potential was realized. At Cambrai, the German defenses were so strong that an artillery bombardment would have destroyed the ground and made it impossible for the infantry to cross. Instead, fleets of tanks flattened barbed wire, crossed enemy trenches, and acted as shields for the advancing infantry. Tanks then played an important role in the allied advances throughout 1918.

BRITISH MARK 1 HEAVY TANK
The first tank to fight in battle was the British Mark 1 tank. Forty nine were ready to fight at the Battle of the Somme on September 15, 1916, but only 18 were reliable enough to take part in the battle itself.

Carried crew of eight men

Total weight of 28 tons (28,450 kg)

Equipped with two 6-pounder guns and four machine guns

PROTECT AND SURVIVE
Leather helmets, faceguards, and chainmail mouthpieces were issued to British tank crews to protect their heads. The visors gave protection against particles of hot metal which flew off the inside of the hull when the tank was hit by a bullet.

Toughened leather skull cap

Leather visor

Chainmail mouthpiece

German A7V tank

A7V TANK
The only German tank built during the war was the huge A7V, a 33-ton (33,500 kg) machine with six machine guns and a crew of 18. Only 20 A7Vs were constructed, and their appearance in the spring of 1918 was too late in the war to make any real impact.

British MarkV tank

INSIDE A TANK

Life inside a tank was very unpleasant. The tank was hot, fume-ridden, and badly ventilated, making the crew sick or even making them faint. The heat was sometimes so great in light tanks that it exploded the ammunition.

Rear entry hatch

Driver's entry hatch

Lid for driver's entry hatch

Driver's visor

T 9171

Iron caterpillar track

The driver and gunner were squashed in the front of the tank

Six men sat cramped around the engine manning the guns

Six-cylinder engine

Machine gun port

BRITISH MARK V TANK

The British Mark V tank first fought in July 1918. It was equipped with two 6-pounder guns and four machine guns, and had a crew of eight. Its advanced system of gears and brakes allowed it to be driven and controlled by only one person.

DRIVING A TANK

The first British tanks were driven by two people, each controlling one track. They had a limited range of 24 miles (40 km) and their tracks regularly broke. Later tanks were driven by a single person and were more maneuverable and robust. They were still vulnerable to enemy shellfire though, and often broke down, as here during the British assault on Arras in April 1917.

CROSSING THE TRENCHES

A tank could cross a narrow trench easily, but it could topple into a wide one. To solve this problem, the British equipped their tanks with circular metal bundles that could be dropped into a trench to form a bridge. Here, a line of Mark V tanks are moving in to attack German trenches in the fall of 1918.

The US enters the war

British medal suggesting the attack on *SS Lusitania* was planned

W HEN WAR broke out in Europe in August 1914, the US remained neutral. The country was deeply divided about the war, since many of its citizens had recently arrived from Europe and were strongly in favor of one side or the other. When German U-boats started to sink American ships, however, public opinion began to turn against Germany. In February 1917 Germany decided to attack all foreign cargo ships to try to reduce supplies to Britain. It also tried to divert US attention from Europe by encouraging its neighbor, Mexico, to invade. This action outraged the US government, and as more US ships were sunk, President Wilson declared war on Germany. This was now a world war.

SS LUSITANIA
On May 7, 1915, the passenger ship *SS Lusitania* was sunk off the coast of Ireland by German torpedoes because the ship was suspected of carrying munitions. The ship was bound from New York to Liverpool, England. Three quarters of the passengers drowned, including 128 US citizens. Their deaths did much to turn the US public against Germany and toward the Allies.

UNCLE SAM
The artist James Montgomery Flagg used himself as a model for Uncle Sam, a cartoon figure intended to represent every American. The portrait was based on Kitchener's similar pose for British recruiting posters (see page 14). Beneath his pointing finger were the words "I WANT YOU FOR THE US ARMY."

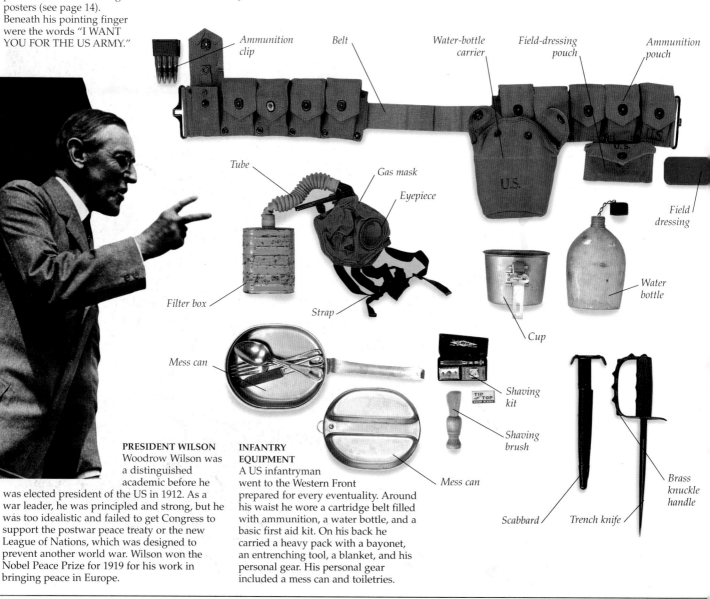

Ammunition clip

Belt

Water-bottle carrier

Field-dressing pouch

Ammunition pouch

Field dressing

Tube

Gas mask

Eyepiece

Filter box

Strap

Cup

Water bottle

Mess can

Shaving kit

Shaving brush

Mess can

Brass knuckle handle

Scabbard

Trench knife

PRESIDENT WILSON
Woodrow Wilson was a distinguished academic before he was elected president of the US in 1912. As a war leader, he was principled and strong, but he was too idealistic and failed to get Congress to support the postwar peace treaty or the new League of Nations, which was designed to prevent another world war. Wilson won the Nobel Peace Prize for 1919 for his work in bringing peace in Europe.

INFANTRY EQUIPMENT
A US infantryman went to the Western Front prepared for every eventuality. Around his waist he wore a cartridge belt filled with ammunition, a water bottle, and a basic first aid kit. On his back he carried a heavy pack with a bayonet, an entrenching tool, a blanket, and his personal gear. His personal gear included a mess can and toiletries.

GUNFIRE

The US First Army saw its first major action on September 12–16, 1918, at St. Mihiel, south of Verdun, France, as a part of a combined Allied attack against German lines. Here an artillery crew fires a 75-mm field gun as a spent shell case flies through the air.

FOR HEROISM

Instituted by Presidential Order in 1918, the Distinguished Service Cross was awarded to someone for extreme heroism against an armed enemy.

Securing strap for pack contents

Haversack

M1905 Springfield bayonet

Entrenching tool

Blanket or greatcoat roll

Assembled pack, US Infantry Equipment

KEEPING IN TOUCH

Many US soldiers had never even left their hometown or state before, and few had ever traveled abroad. Stationed in France, in a country where they could not speak the language, many became very homesick. They wrote letters to their families and friends, and received letters, postcards, and food packages in return.

Under enemy lines

FOR MUCH OF the war on the Western Front, the two sides faced each other in rows of heavily fortified trenches. These massive defenses were very difficult to overcome, so engineers found ways of undermining them. The British army recruited coal miners and "clay kickers," who used to dig tunnels for the London subway system. The Germans had their own miners. Both excavated tunnels and mines deep under enemy lines and packed them with explosives, ready to be detonated when an attack began. Countermines were also dug to cut into and destroy enemy mines before they could be finished. The opposing miners sometimes met and fought in underground battles. Vast mines were exploded by the British at the Battle of the Somme on July 1, 1916, but their most effective use was under Messines Ridge at the start of the Battle of Passchendaele.

TO THE RESCUE
A gas attack or a shell burst near a tunnel entrance could fill the mine with fumes, suffocating the men working inside. This German breathing apparatus was kept on standby for use by rescue parties.

Air tubes

SAPPERS AT WORK
British artist David Bomberg's painting shows members of the Royal Engineers, known as sappers, digging and reinforcing an underground trench. Sappers ensured that trenches and tunnels were properly constructed and did not collapse.

Headpiece

Straps to hol mouthpiece i place

Nose clip

Air tube

Breathing ba was carried on chest

Air from oxyge cylinders carried on the back entered the breathin bag throug this valve

OXYGEN RELIEF
This British breathing apparatus is similar to the German equipment on the left. Compressed oxygen contained in the breathing bags was released through the air tubes to help the miner breathe.

Background picture: One of many British mines explodes under German lines at the Battle of the Somme, July 1, 1916

> *"It is horrible. You often wish you were dead, there is no shelter, we are lying in water ... our clothes do not dry."*
>
> GERMAN SOLDIER, PASSCHENDAELE, 1917

WATERLOGGED
The water table around Ypres was very high, so the trenches were built above ground by banking up soil and sand bangs. Even so, the trenches were constantly flooded. Pumping out mines and trenches, as these Australian tunnelers are doing at Hooge, Belgium, during September 1917, was an essential, never-ending task.

Passchendaele

During 1917, the British planned a massive attack against the German front line around Ypres, Belgium. They aimed to break into Belgium and capture the channel ports, stopping the German submarines from using them as a base to attack British shipping. The battle began on June 7, 1917. After a huge artillery bombardment, 19 mines packed with 1 million tons of explosive blew up simultaneously under the German lines on Messines Ridge. The noise could be heard in London 140 miles (220 km) away. The ridge was soon captured, but the British failed to take quick advantage. Heavy rainfall in August and October turned the battlefield into a muddy wasteland. The village and ridge of Passchendaele were eventually captured on November 10, 1917, only to be lost again the following March. In summer of 1918, the Allies recaptured and kept the ground.

MUDDY QUAGMIRE
Heavy rainfall and constant shelling at Passchendaele created a deadly mudbath. Many injured men died as they were unable to lift themselves clear of the cloying mud. Stretcher bearers were barely able to carry the wounded to dressing stations. The British poet Siegfried Sassoon, wrote that "I died in hell – (They called it Passchendaele)."

Below: British troops moving forward over shell-torn terrain during the Battle of Passchendaele

The final year

IN EARLY 1918, the war looked to be turning in favor of Germany and its allies. Russia had withdrawn from the war, enabling Germany to concentrate its efforts on the Western Front, and US troops had yet to arrive in France in any great numbers. A vast offensive in March brought German troops to within 40 miles (64 km) of Paris. But behind the lines, Germany was far from strong. The Allied blockade of German ports meant that the country was short of vital supplies. The railroad network was collapsing through lack of maintenance, and food was short. Strikes and even mutinies became common. Elsewhere, Ottoman Turkey and Bulgaria collapsed in the face of Allied attacks, while the Italians scored a decisive victory against Austria-Hungary. By early November, Germany stood alone. On November 7, a German delegation crossed the front line to discuss peace terms with the Allies. The war was almost over.

NEW LEADER
In 1917, Vladimir Lenin, the leader of the Bolshevik (Communist) Party, became the new ruler of Russia. He was opposed to the war, and ordered an immediate cease-fire when he came to power.

German and Russian troops celebrating the cease-fire on the Eastern Front, 1917

Russia pulls out

The Russian government became increasingly unpopular as the war progressed. The army was demoralized by constant defeats, and by early 1917, there was large-scale fraternization with German troops along the Eastern Front. In February 1917, a revolution overthrew the czar, but the new government continued the war. A second revolution in October brought the Bolshevik Party to power. A cease-fire was agreed with Germany, and in March 1918 Russia signed the Treaty of Brest-Litovsk and withdrew from the war.

THE LUDENDORFF OFFENSIVE
On March 21, 1918, General Ludendorff launched a huge attack on the Western Front. He hoped to defeat Britain and France before US reinforcements could arrive. The attack took the Allies by surprise, and Germany advanced by almost 40 miles (64 km) by July, but at the heavy cost of 500,000 casualties.

French and British troops in action during the Ludendorff Offensive

January 8 US President Wilson issues 14 Points for Peace
March 3 Treaty of Brest-Litovsk – Russia leaves the war
March 21 Vast German Ludendorff offensive on the Western Front
July 15 Last German offensive launched on Western Front
July 18 French counterattack begins on the Marne
August 8 British launch offensive near Amiens
September 12 Americans launch offensive at St. Mihiel
September 14 Allies attack Bulgarians at Salonika
September 25 Bulgaria seeks peace
September 27 British begin to breach Hindenburg Line

BATTLE OF THE MARNE

On July 18, 1918, French and US forces, led by General Foch, counterattacked against the German advance on the Marne River, east of Paris. They stopped the German offensive in its tracks and began to push the Germans back eastward. By August 6, the Germans had lost 168,000 men, many buried where they fell on the battlefields (left). The tide of battle had at last turned decisively in favor of the Allied armies.

French soldiers identifying German dead before burial

CROSSING THE LINE

On August 8, 1918, a massive British offensive began near Amiens. The German army was increasingly short of men and vital supplies, including food, and so gave little resistance. The Allied troops continued to push forward toward the heavily fortified Hindenburg Line. On September 29, the British 46th North Midland Division captured the bridge at Riqueval, over the St. Quentin Canal. They posed for a celebratory photograph, because they had broken the Line at last.

Many French children did not remember life before the German occupation of their towns and cities

Background picture: German troops advancing at the Somme, April 1918

French children march alongside the Allied army

THE LAST DAYS

By October 5, the Allied armies had breached the entire Hindenburg Line and were crossing open country. Both sides suffered great casualties as the German army was pushed steadily eastward. The British and French recaptured towns and cities lost in 1914, including Lille (left), and by early November 1918 they recaptured Mons, where they had fired the first shots of the war in August 1914. By now, the German retreat was turning into a rout.

September 28 German commander Ludendorff advises the Kaiser to seek peace as army crumbles
October 1 British capture Ottoman Turkish-held Damascus

October 6 German government starts to negotiate an armistice
October 21 Czechoslovakia declares its independence
October 24 Italian army begins

decisive battle of Vittorio-Veneto against Austria-Hungary
October 29 German fleet mutinies
October 30 Ottoman Turkey agrees an armistice

November 4 Austria-Hungary agrees an armistice
November 9 The Kaiser abdicates
November 11 Armistice between Germany and the Allies; war ends

Armistice and peace

CARRIAGE TALKS
On November 7, 1918, a German delegation headed by a government minister, Matthias Erzberger, crossed the front line to meet the Allied commander-in-chief, Marshal Foch, in his railroad carriage in the forest of Compiègne. At 5 am on November 11, the two sides signed an armistice agreement to come into effect six hours later.

AT 11 AM ON THE 11th day of the 11th month of 1918, the guns of Europe fell silent after more than four years of war. The problems of war were now replaced by the equally pressing problems of peace. Germany had asked for an armistice (cease-fire) in order to discuss a possible peace treaty. It had not surrendered, but its soldiers were surrendering in hordes and its navy had mutinied. The Allies wanted to make sure that Germany would never go to war again. The eventual peace treaty redrew the map of Europe and forced Germany to pay massive damages to the Allies. German armed forces were reduced in size and strength, and Germany lost a great deal of land and all of its overseas colonies.

The New York Times.

ARMISTICE SIGNED, END OF THE WAR!
BERLIN SEIZED BY REVOLUTIONISTS;
NEW CHANCELLOR BEGS FOR ORDER;
OUSTED KAISER FLEES TO HOLLAND

DISPLACED PEOPLE
Many refugees, like these Lithuanians, were displaced during the war. The end of hostilities allowed thousands of refugees – mainly French, Belgians, Italians, and Serbians whose lands had been occupied by the Central Powers – to return home to their newly liberated countries. In addition, there were as many as 6.5 million prisoners of war who needed to be repatriated. This complex task was finally achieved by the fall of 1919.

SPREADING THE NEWS
News of the armistice spread around the world in minutes. It was reported in newspapers and typed out in telegrams, while word-of-mouth spread the joyous news to each and every member of the local neighborhood.

VIVE LA PAIX!
In Paris (below), French, British, and American soldiers joined Parisians in an impromptu procession through the city. In London, women and children danced in the streets, while their men prepared to return from the front. In Germany, the news was greeted with a mixture of shock and relief that the fighting was at last over.

SIGNING THE TREATY
These soldiers watching the signing of the Treaty of Versailles had waited a long time for this moment. The Allies first met their German counterparts in January 1919. The Americans wanted a fair and just treaty that guaranteed democracy and freedom to all people, while both France and to a lesser extent Britain wanted to keep Germany weak and divided. Negotiations almost broke down several times before a final agreement was reached in June 1919.

THE TREATY OF VERSAILLES
The peace treaty that ended the war was signed in the Hall of Mirrors in the Palace of Versailles near Paris, on June 28, 1919. Sir William Orpen's painting shows the four Allied leaders watching the German delegates sign the treaty ending German imperial power in Europe, just 48 years after the German Empire had been proclaimed in the same hall.

THE PEACE TREATIES
The Treaty of Versailles was signed by representatives of the Allied powers and Germany. The Allies signed subsequent treaties elsewhere in Paris with Austria in September 1919, Bulgaria in November 1919, Turkey in April 1920, and Hungary in June 1920. By then, a new map of Europe had emerged.

The Treaty of Versailles

General Foch — Georges Clemenceau — David Lloyd George — Vittorio Orlando — Giorgio Sonnino

THE VICTORIOUS ALLIES
The negotiations in Paris were dominated by French premier Georges Clemenceau (supported by General Foch), British premier David Lloyd George, Italian premier Vittorio Orlando – seen here with his foreign minister, Giorgio Sonnino – and the US president Woodrow Wilson. Together the Big Four, as the leaders became known, thrashed out the main details of the peace settlement.

The cost of the war

THE COST OF THE World War I in human lives is unimaginable. More than 65 million men fought, of whom more than half were killed or injured – 8 million killed, 2 million died of illness and disease, 21.2 million wounded, and 7.8 million taken prisoner or missing. In addition, about 6.6 million civilians perished. Among the combatant nations, with the exception of the US, there was barely a family that had not lost at least one son or brother; some had lost every male member. Entire towns and villages were wiped off the map, and fertile farmland was turned into a deathly bogland. Financially, the economies of Europe were ruined, while the US emerged as a major world power. Not surprisingly, at the end of 1918, people hoped they would never again have to experience the slaughter and destruction they had lived through for the past four years.

ONE LIFE
A soldier stands on Pilckem Ridge during the Battle of Passchendaele in August 1917. The crudely made cross indicates a hastily dug grave, but many soldiers were engulfed by the mud and their graves remained unmarked.

THE UNKNOWN SOLDIER
Many of the dead were so badly disfigured that it was impossible to identify them. Plain crosses mark their graves. Thousands more just disappeared, presumed dead. Both France and Britain ceremoniously buried one unknown warrior – at the Arc de Triomphe, Paris, and Westminster Abbey, London.

AFTER CARE
The war left thousands of soldiers disfigured and disabled. Reconstructive surgery was carried out to repair facial damage, but masks were used to cover the most horrific disfigurement. Artificial limbs gave many disabled soldiers some mobility. But the horrors of the war remained forever.

Some soldiers stayed in nursing homes for the rest of their lives

Many soldiers painted to pass the time

Background picture: Poppies in the battlefields of northern France

WAR MEMORIALS

The entire length of the Western Front is marked with graveyards and memorials to those who lost their lives in the war. At Verdun, the French national mausoleum and ossuary (burial vault) at Douaumont (below) contains the remains of 130,000 unidentified French and German soldiers. There are 410 British cemeteries in the Somme valley alone.

Prussian Iron Cross

Victoria Cross (V.C.)

MEMENTOS

A profusion of flowers, including red Flanders poppies, grew along both sides of the Western Front. Soldiers, such as Private Jack Mudd of the 214 Battalion of the London Regiment (above), would press them as mementos to send home to their loved ones. Mudd sent this poppy to his wife Lizzie before he was killed, in 1917, in the Battle of Passchendaele. Canadian doctor, John McCrae, wrote the poem *In Flanders Fields* after tending wounded soldiers near Ypres in 1915. His mention of poppies in the poem inspired the British Legion to sell paper poppies to raise money for injured soldiers, and as a sign of remembrance for the dead.

FOR GALLANTRY

Every combatant nation awarded military and civilian medals to honor bravery. Five million Iron Crosses were given to German soldiers and their allies. Over two million Croix de Guerre were issued to French soldiers, military units, civilians, and towns, and 576 Victoria Crosses, Britain's highest award, were presented to British and Empire troops.

French *Croix de Guerre*

Index

Acknowledgments

**Dorling Kindersley and the author
would like to thank:**
Elizabeth Bowers, Christopher Dowling,
Laurie Milner, Mark Pindelski, and the
photography archive team at the Imperial
War Museum for their invaluable help;
Right Section, Kings Own Royal Horse
Artillery for firing the gun shown on
page 10.
Editorial assistance: Carey Scott
Index: Lynn Bresler

**The publishers would also like to thank
the following for their kind permission
to reproduce their photographs:**
a=above, b=below, c=center l=left,
r=right, t=top

AKG London: 6l, 7crb, 36br, 37bl, 38cl,
38bl, 41tr, 42c, 42bl, 43br, 38cl, 38bl, 41tr,
42c, 42bl, 43br, 52cl, 58–59t, 60c; **Andrew
L. Chernack, Springfield, Pennsylvania**:
3tr, 55tr; **Corbis**: 2tr, 6tr, 7tr, 20tr, 22tr,
31tr; Bettmann 8tr, 26–27, 44–45c, 49bl,
55tr, 35bc, 49tl, 54bl, 55t, 55br, 58–59,
61cr; Dave G. Houser 41cr; **Robert
Harding Picture Library**: 63c; **Heeres-
geschichtliches Museum, Wien**: 8bl;
Hulton Getty: 14tl, 17tl, 19br, 21br, 33tr,
32–33b, 35clb, 36cra, 41c, 43t, 47cra,
50clb, 51cl, 58tl, 60tl, 60b, 61tr, 61b;
Topical Press Agency 50cl; **Imperial War
Museum**: 2tl, 2cr, 8tl, 9bl, 11tr, 10–11t,
12clb, 13cl, 14bc, 15tr, 15cr, 16c, 16b,
17br, 18tr, 18cl, cr, 18br, *The Menin Road*,
1918, by Paul Nash 19tr, 19cla, 19cr,

19clb, 20bl, 20br, 21tc, 21tr, 22bca, 22bl,
23t, 23br, 24tl, 24c, 26bl, 27tl, 27bc,
26–27b, 28cl, 28cr, 29tr, 29br, 28–29b,
30tr, 30cl, 31br, 32l, 32c, 33tl, 33cr, 35cb,
35bl, 34–35c, 36clb, 37, 38tl, 38tr, 39cr,
39br, 40cl, 40br, 41tl, 41b, 45br, 44–45b,
48cr, 48bl, 50bc, 51tr, 51c, 52bl, 53cr,
53br, 54tl, 56cl, 57tr, 57cr, 56–57b,
56–57c, 58b, 59tr, 59b, *The Signing of
Peace in the Hall of Mirrors, Versailles*,
1919–20, by Sir William Orpen 61tl, 62tl,
62c; **David King Collection**: 46bl, 47tl,
58cla; **National Army Museum**: 44bl;
National Gallery Of Canada, Ottawa:
Transfer from the Canadian War
Memorials, *Dazzle ships in dry dock at
Liverpool*, 1921, by Edward Wadsworth
39tl; **Peter Newark's Military Pictures**:

13ac, 42tr; **RAF Museum, Hendon**:
34cla, 34cl; **Roger-Viollet**: 9tr, 9cr, 11br,
13cr, 19tl; Boyer 17bl; **Spink and Son
Ltd**: 3tl, 4tr, 43bc; **Telegraph Colour
Library**: J.P. Fruchet 62c; **Topham
Picturepoint**: 42tl, 46tl, 47br, 46–47b,
62b; ASAP 43cl; **Ullstein Bild**: 8–9c, 46tr.

Jacket credits:
AKG London: back cra, back bl;
Imperial War Museum: back tl, back br,
front tl, front c, front cra, front b (staged
image), inside front bl, spine b; **Topham
Picturepoint**: front cl.

**All other images © Dorling Kindersley.
For further information see:**
www.dkimages.com

THE VALUE OF CARING

The Story of Eleanor Roosevelt

VALUE COMMUNICATIONS, INC.
PUBLISHERS
LA JOLLA, CALIFORNIA

THE VALUE OF CARING

The Story of
Eleanor Roosevelt

BY ANN DONEGAN JOHNSON

THE DANBURY PRESS

The Value of Caring is part of the ValueTales series.

The Value of Caring text copyright © 1977
by Ann Donegan Johnson. Illustrations copyright © 1977
by Value Communications, Inc.

First Edition
Manufactured in the United States of America
For information write to: ValueTales, P.O. Box 1012
La Jolla, CA 92038

Library of Congress Cataloging in Publication Data

Johnson, Ann Donegan.
    The value of caring.

    (ValueTales)
    SUMMARY: A biography of the First Lady who not
only aided her husband after he was stricken with polio but
also served as a delegate to the United Nations where she
helped start UNICEF.
    1.   Roosevelt, Eleanor Roosevelt, 1884–1962—Juvenile
literature. 2.   Presidents—United States—Wives—
Biography—Juvenile literature. [1.   Roosevelt,
Eleanor Roosevelt, 1884–1962. 2.   First ladies.
3.   Kindness]   I.   Title.
E807.1.J63   973.917′092′4 [B] [92]   77-6656

ISBN 0-916392-11-2

This tale is about Eleanor Roosevelt, a caring woman. The story that follows is based on events in her life. More historical facts about Eleanor Roosevelt can be found on page 63.

Once upon a time...

there was a very happy woman named Eleanor Roosevelt. She had everything a woman could want. She had a fine husband and beautiful, healthy children, and she lived in a lovely big house.

But in spite of all the wonderful things she had, Eleanor was sometimes a bit shy and timid.

Of course she was never shy when she was having fun with her family. All summer long she watched her children swim in the sea near their home. Sometimes she and her husband went sailing in their boat.

Eleanor was proud of her husband Franklin. She was sure that he would do important things someday. But just when it seemed that she was most happy and most proud, a very sad thing happened.

Franklin caught a dreaded disease called polio. There were no shots to protect people against polio in those days, so many persons were crippled by this sickness. Eleanor thought of this as she nursed her husband.

"Franklin is so ill," she said to herself. "Perhaps he will never walk again. Oh how miserable that could make him!"

Eleanor went off by herself to think. "I'm afraid," thought Eleanor, "just like I used to be when I was a little girl. And I used to be lonely, too. But then I had a make-believe friend who cheered me up."

"You still have a make-believe friend," said a small voice near Eleanor.

1920 NY

"Oh my!" said Eleanor, seeing a little girl who looked the way Eleanor herself had looked when she was small. "My make-believe friend! And how blue you are! But then, I'm in a very sad mood today. You look just like I feel."

Then Eleanor remembered being a timid, fearful little girl. She remembered the first time her make-believe friend had come to her.

"Why are you so unhappy, Eleanor?" her make-believe friend asked.

"Because I'm lonesome," said Eleanor. "I have no one to play with."

"I'll play with you," said her make-believe friend.

"Will you?" said Eleanor. "Do you like me?" She knew that her little friend existed only in her mind, but she was still a comfort to Eleanor.

"I'm not beautiful like my mother and my aunts," Eleanor told her make-believe friend. "I'm sort of plain, and I'm clumsy. My mother says I'm so serious and old-fashioned that she ought to call me Granny. And my aunts laugh when she says this. I think they like to tease me!"

"But Granny is a nice name," said Eleanor's make-believe friend. "In fact, I'd like it if you'd call *me* Granny!"

"All right," said Eleanor. "I have to call you something, and it is nice to have someone to talk with. But I wish I were beautiful, like my mother."

"Don't you know that you *are* beautiful?" said Granny. "Beauty isn't just being pretty. Beauty is caring about other people and showing that you care!"

Eleanor felt better then. She felt still better when Granny
stayed with her at night so that she wouldn't be afraid of
the dark.

"Darkness is nothing to be scared about," said Granny.
"It's just what happens when you put the lamp out."

Soon Eleanor was so brave that she and Granny could
even go down into the unlighted cellar.

With Granny to cheer her on, Eleanor learned to do other hard things. She practiced walking with a book on her head so that she would be more graceful. She was always neat and clean, so that people would like to have her around.

And Granny always reminded Eleanor that caring for others would make her feel better about herself.

It did make her feel better to care for others, although she was still shy with some people. But she was always happy and comfortable when she was with her father. He was pleased when he saw her becoming a warm and caring person.

"If you can let people know you love them, you'll make them happy," he told her. "That will make you happy too."

Eleanor remembered her father's advice when she traveled with her family to the far-off country of Italy. She was riding a donkey, and she saw that the servant boy who led her donkey was limping.

"You ride," said Eleanor, getting off the donkey. "Your feet are sore and you need a rest."

"No one else has ever seemed to care how I felt," said the boy. "You're a very special little girl."

19

When she grew older Eleanor went away to school. Of course Granny went along.

"You'll have a good time here," said Granny, "because you care about your classmates."

Eleanor did have a good time, and she wasn't nearly as shy as she had been.

After she finished school, an absolutely wonderful thing happened to Eleanor. She met a handsome young man named Franklin Roosevelt, and she found that she cared about him in a very special way. What's more, he cared about her too.

"Do you really like me," asked Eleanor, "even though I'm not as pretty as the other girls?"

"I like you best," he answered.

In fact, Franklin fell in love with Eleanor and asked her to marry him.

Their wedding was beautiful. Eleanor's uncle came to see them get married, and everyone stared at him. That's because her uncle was Teddy Roosevelt, president of the United States.

Eleanor didn't care how people stared at her uncle. She was too happy. She was marrying Franklin, and she knew that their life together would be wonderful. It was, too. It was very wonderful—until the sad time when Franklin got polio.

"Oh Granny," said Eleanor, as she remembered her joyful wedding day. "We've been so happy together. Now I'm afraid that Franklin will have so many problems because of his illness. I've got to find a way to help him."

Franklin did have problems. Even after he was well again, his legs remained paralyzed. Eleanor was sad, but she remembered how caring about others had helped her with her own problems.

"Why don't you run for public office?" Eleanor asked Franklin. "I think you'd be happier if you were doing something to help others."

"How can I run for office?" he said. "I can't even walk properly."

"You can do everything that's really important," she told him. "Don't worry. I'll help you, and you'll be the next governor of New York state!"

Do you think that's what happened?

Indeed, that's exactly what happened. Franklin won the election.

"I'm glad I won," he told Eleanor, "but I've taken on a tough job. A lot of people are depending on me."

"Let me help," she said. "Together we can do it."

Eleanor and Franklin did work together, and they were a perfect team. Franklin stayed in his office, while Eleanor went out to talk with the people, to find out what they needed most. She went places and did things that few women had ever done before.

Granny went with her, but even Granny was a bit nervous the first time they got on an airplane.

"G-g-gee this is exciting," said Granny. "Most people have never ridden in an airplane. Are you sure we should try it?"

"I'm sure as can be," laughed Eleanor, and away they went.

With Eleanor's help Franklin solved many problems for the people of New York. But then the hard times called the Great Depression came to America.

Factories shut down and stores went out of business.
Farmers stopped growing food and banks had no money. All
over the country people lost their jobs.

Everyone was frightened and worried. When the time came to elect a new president, the people wanted to vote for someone who cared about those who were out of work and out of money.

Whom did most of them vote for?

Why they voted for Franklin Roosevelt, of course.

Franklin gave the people new hope. On the day he became president he told them, "We have nothing to fear but fear itself."

He meant that no matter how bad things were, it did no good to be afraid. Eleanor had helped him to believe in himself, so that he could work to overcome his polio. He wanted the people to have faith that they could work to solve their problems, too.

Because Franklin became president, Eleanor was now known as the first lady. She greeted guests who came to the White House, and she appeared at many public events.

"Is this all you're going to do?" said Granny. "Aren't you going to go out and see people and find out what they need?"

"Why naturally I'm going to do that," said Eleanor.

She did more than see the people. She let the people know that she and Franklin really cared about their problems. There was no television in those days, but there were lots of newspapers. Eleanor talked with reporters every chance she got.

Eleanor didn't just talk. She did things, and she went places where no other first lady had dreamed of going. Granny went along and always had a very good time. At least she did until the day she and Eleanor went down into a dark, dangerous coal mine.

"This is very thrilling," said Granny. "I think perhaps it's too thrilling. We could be home in the nice, safe White House, you know. We don't really belong here."

"Certainly we belong here," said Eleanor as she shook hands with the miners. "We belong wherever we're needed."

When Franklin ran for a second term as president, Eleanor helped all she could.

"The people want a president who will work with them to help solve their problems," she told Franklin. "You want to keep on doing everything you can for as many people as possible."

Eleanor and Franklin traveled all over the country on a special campaign train, so that even people in little towns could see that the president and the first lady cared about them.

The people trusted Franklin and he was reelected. But before long his job became harder than ever. Do you know why?

37

Because one bright Sunday morning, enemy planes suddenly dropped bombs on the American ships that were anchored at Pearl Harbor, a big navy base in Hawaii.

Now the United States had to fight in the great war that had already been going on in other parts of the world.

39

Eleanor soon began to travel to the places where American soldiers were fighting.

She visited the wounded and tried to make them feel better.

"You've certainly changed," said Granny. "Do you remember how shy and fearful you used to be? You aren't a bit shy any more."

"I guess not," said Eleanor. "I don't really have time to be shy. I'm too busy talking to people. Besides, when I'm caring for others I forget to be afraid or to worry about myself."

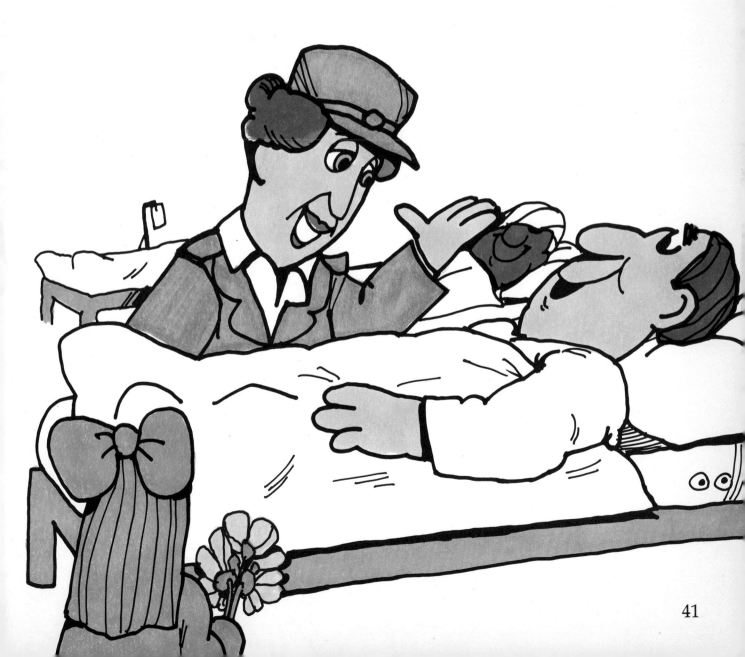

Eleanor didn't just visit the troops and then forget about them. When she got home from her trips, she wrote or telephoned the families of the men she'd seen.

"I saw your son," she told one family on the phone.
"He's fine but he wants you to send him some
chocolate chip cookies."

"Say, ask them to send me some too," whispered Granny.

Millions of men and women worked in factories making things to help win the war. Eleanor visited them too, and Granny always tagged along.

The people who worked in the factories were happy
to see Eleanor when she came.

They were even happier when at last the war came to
an end.

It was a glad time in America, but it was a sad time too. For Franklin himself did not live to see the end of the war. He died just before peace came again. All over the country flags flew at half-mast to show how the American people would miss their president.

Eleanor was no longer first lady. She was alone
again. She had lost the one she cared about the most.

"Now I must decide what I'll do with the rest of my life,"
she said to Granny and to Fala, Franklin's little dog.

47

First she went to be with her grandchildren.

"Oh, boy!" they cried, for they loved her very much. "Now you have time to play with us."

But when she saw her own happy, healthy grandchildren, Eleanor knew that there was still work for her to do. "It would be nice to stay with you," she said, "but there are boys and girls in the world who have no place to live and not enough to eat. I must try to help them. Many of them have no one else who cares about them."

And so she began to treat all the world's children as if they were her own.

Many people had lost their homes in the war. They were called refugees and lived in crowded camps in far-away countries. They felt afraid. "Everyone has forgotten us," they said.

But Eleanor went to see them, to find out what they needed most. Then she returned home and spoke about the problems of these homeless people and their lonely, uncared-for children.

The refugee children were not the only ones who needed help. In some lands there were thousands of youngsters who didn't have enough to eat. Eleanor set her mind to finding ways to help them.

And then she had a wonderful idea.

She began to work in the United Nations to help the sad, poor, and hungry people everywhere.

"You may not be first lady of the United States anymore," said Granny happily, "but now everyone knows that you're first lady of the world."

Eleanor also found children in the United States who were in need.

The schools on some Indian reservations had closed because there wasn't enough money to pay the teachers. Eleanor helped raise money to open the Indian schools again. And because of Eleanor many other people began working to help these young Americans.

Eleanor also realized that black children weren't treated as well as white children, so she spoke out. She called for new laws so that all children would have an equal chance.

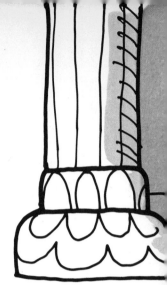

"Slow down!" cried Granny as Eleanor ran up the steps of the Capitol building on her way to talk with the lawmakers. "Wait for me!"

"Sorry," said Eleanor, "but the rights of children are very important. I have to make the congressmen see that. I can't slow down."

Eleanor never really did slow down. She spent the rest of her life working for others. And all sorts of people— kings and presidents, the powerful and the powerless, the wise and the foolish—came to her for advice.